A Totally
KILLER
Wedding

LARGE
PRINT
EDITION

Totally
80s
Mysteries
Book 1

Books by D.A. Wilkerson

Totally 80s Mysteries

A Totally Killer Wedding
Most Likely to Kill
Of Heist and Men
A Totally 80s Christmas

Mystery Journals

Mysterious Musings
My Totally Suspect Notebook

A Totally KILLER Wedding

D.A. Wilkerson
Mystery Author
danawilkerson.com

A Totally Killer Wedding: Large Print Edition
Totally 80s Mysteries Book 1
by D.A. Wilkerson

Published by Dana Wilkerson, LLC
Edmond, OK
danawilkerson.com

First Edition: April 2022

Large Print Paperback ISBN: 978-1-948148-70-2
Paperback ISBN: 978-1-948148-30-6
eBook ISBN: 978-1-948148-31-3

Dedicated to my hometown of Montgomery City, Missouri, and all the people I grew up with there in the 80s

ONE

I CLASPED MY HANDS in front of my chest as the opening strains of "Here Comes the Bride" seeped around the thick sanctuary doors into the foyer of First Community Church. Two ushers pushed open the double doors from the inside, revealing the petal-strewn aisle, a few hundred packed-in guests rising from the pews, and the most stunning man in Cherry County, Missouri, gazing right at me.

He raised an eyebrow as I stood motionless for a few seconds until someone nudged me not so subtly. I jerked to attention. As I lurched aside to let the bride and her father walk down the aisle, a blush started at the neckline of my new red, orange, and yellow floral dress. The heat moved upward until my face could have doubled as a stop sign.

The bride's princess dress with gigantic, puffed sleeves and even bigger, newly permed long blonde hair instantly blocked my view. The ushers stepped inside the sanctuary and firmly shut the doors behind them. I noted the glare one of them gave me before he disappeared. After the wedding, I would apologize to the bride. For now, I had to wait.

The church foyer was dotted with ornately framed mirrors, as some well-meaning deacon's wife had once heard mirrors make a space look bigger. I took advantage of the one nearest me and checked my naturally curly auburn hair to ensure my hairspray was holding up.

I dropped into one of the plush, country-blue wingback chairs flanking the oversized double doors that led outside, and I stuck my bright red pinky nail between my teeth. Within seconds, I jerked my finger with its freshly attached press-on nail from my mouth and sat on my hand to protect it from myself.

My mind wandered to the man at the end of the aisle. Not the groom—his best man. The two had inherited the tall, blue-eyed Patrick family genes, but the older brother took the attractiveness level up a notch with his toned body, devilish grin, and a hint of bad-boy attitude.

Aidan Patrick was nearing forty, but the man could still fill out a tux. He had also been my aunt Starla's high school sweetheart, which meant he was off-limits. That was for the best, as he'd never be interested in me—a slightly overweight church secretary with a limp. I thought I was a catch, but he wouldn't. He also swapped out girlfriends at a staggering pace, which was not what I was looking for.

I wasn't invited to the Burns-Patrick wedding, but anytime a large, non-church-sanctioned event happened at First Comm, a staff member or deacon had to be on site at all times. This wedding might well be the event of the year in Cherry Hill, so I volunteered. Plus, I knew this church better than my own home, so if anyone needed anything, I'd be able to provide it with ease.

My lifelong best friend Trixie was less than delighted when I told her about the wedding, as we had planned to spend the day celebrating our twenty-eighth birthdays. When she awoke to the most beautiful March day, she was undoubtedly even more annoyed. Instead of enjoying a nice lunch with friends at Dino's, a totally fabulous Italian restaurant overlooking nearby Lake of the Ozarks, she was likely down the street chasing her two kids around the park.

With nothing better to do, I reached over and picked up a wedding program from a marble-topped accent table. "March 23, 1985" was emblazoned at the top, followed by the couple's names: Miss Blair Burns and Dr. Shane Patrick. I skimmed through the names of their attendants and family members.

Blair wasn't from Cherry Hill, so I didn't know

anyone on her side, including her eight—*eight*—bridesmaids. I did, however, recognize a few of the groomsmen's names, and I knew all of Shane's immediate family. Shane was several years ahead of me in school, so I wouldn't call us friends, but in a town of 3,224, you're acquainted with most everybody.

I wondered why the wedding was here at the Patrick family's church instead of in Blair's hometown, since typically weddings are held at the bride's church. However, First Comm was the biggest and prettiest church in town. The stately building boasted stained-glass windows, a pipe organ, a towering steeple, prime real estate in Cherry Hill's charming downtown, and a large parking lot. Those factors may have contributed to the decision.

Shane opened his own medical practice in Cherry Hill six months ago, after working at the hospital in Jefferson City for a few years. He and Blair made a pretense of living separately. Their home included a detached three-car garage with an apartment on the second floor. Shane was supposedly camping out there while Blair lived in the house, but everyone knew they both lived in the house. There had been no small amount of tongue-wagging around the church about it.

When the couple asked to hold the wedding at First

Comm with Pastor Coker officiating, the deacons held a closed-door meeting about the appropriateness of our beloved pastor's seeming approval of Shane and Blair's living situation. My guess was the deacons caved purely because even though the couple didn't often attend church, they did give a hefty tithe.

The warbling sounds of an older woman butchering "Time After Time" drifted into the foyer. Cyndi Lauper she wasn't. I would never be able to enjoy that song again. As the last note died away, I pushed to my feet, crossed to the double doors leading into the sanctuary, and peeked through the crack between them. Shane and Blair were preparing to say their vows. The ceremony would be over in a few minutes.

Not wanting to be the center of attention again when the doors opened, I moved to the side of the foyer. A side door burst open and a woman rushed toward me. "Quick! The mother of the bride needs some tissues!"

I opened the antique armoire beside me and whipped out a fresh box, nearly hitting her face with it in my hurry. For the second time in less than thirty minutes, I was on the receiving end of a glare. The woman did mutter a quick thank you as she dashed back through the door.

Within minutes, the doors pushed open as the organist pulled out all the stops for the "Wedding

March." "Daaah-daaah-duh-dah-dah-dah-dah," I sang aloud without realizing until the same usher from earlier shot me another glare. I gave him a sheepish look while continuing my "dahs" in my head as the bride and groom swept through the foyer and out into the spring sunshine.

Next came the matron of honor and Aidan, who gave me a wink as he passed by. I couldn't help but grin back.

The bride's parents followed the rest of the wedding party. Her mother was wiping her eyes, but she was alert enough to spot me and make a beeline across the foyer. "Would you be a darling and fix me a glass of lemonade? Thank you." I struggled to stop my mouth from gaping open at the strange and specific request. Before I could respond, she was tugging Mr. Burns out the door.

———

"BECKETT? WHAT are you doing?"

There was no mistaking that southern drawl. My face burned again as I backed my top half out of a giant cabinet in the church kitchen. From my knees, I peered up at Greg Villanova, First Comm's new youth pastor. "Looking for the lemonade. It has to be in here somewhere."

"You mean *this* lemonade?" He pointed to a clear, plastic jar filled with pink powder with "LEMONADE" scrawled on it in permanent marker.

Mmm. I closed my eyes and thought about the scent of permanent marker. I could almost smell it in my head.

"Beckett!"

My eyes popped open. "Yes. The lemonade. Guess I was looking for yellow lemonade, not pink. I forgot we ran out of yellow."

Greg reached his hand out to me. I shot him a confused look and shook it.

He sighed. "No. Let me help you up."

I grabbed his hand and he hauled me to my feet.

"What are you doing here?" I asked. "You didn't have to come to the wedding."

"Some of the high school boys are coming over to my house tonight to watch the latest *Indiana Jones* movie. I thought I'd raid the church's stash so they don't eat up my entire paycheck."

"Becky, do you have that lemonade yet? Mrs. Burns won't shut up about it." Aidan rounded the corner into the kitchen and stopped short. He grinned and leaned against the doorframe. "Sorry to interrupt."

I glanced down. Greg hadn't yet let go of my hand.

I dropped it as yet another blush crept up my neck.

"Greg was helping me up. And I go by Beckett now. I have for years." Beckett, my mom's maiden name, was my official first name. When I was a baby, she always called me Beckett, but everyone else called me Becky. Uncharacteristically, Mom gave in and joined them. Like her, I loved my full name, so when I moved away after high school, I decided that was a great time to start using it.

"Your time in the big city of St. Louis made you decide to be all fancy?"

Greg interjected, "Hey, I don't know who—"

I cut him off. "It's fine. I've known Aidan my entire life. He used to date my aunt."

"Used to?" Aidan raised one eyebrow. How did he do that? I tried it myself and failed so spectacularly he and I both laughed.

"Now about that lemonade ..." Aidan said.

"Let me whip some up. Won't take a minute." I grabbed a pitcher from the counter, measured out some powder, stuck it under the tap, and swirled it around while it filled.

I turned to Aidan. "What did you mean by 'used to'?"

He smirked, nodded at the sink, and said, "You might want to watch what you're doing."

Lemonade poured over the top of the pitcher and through my fingers. I turned off the water and shook the sticky drink from my hand. Greg held out an ice-filled Styrofoam cup for me to fill and then handed it to Aidan as I rinsed and dried my hands.

"Thanks, *Beckett*. Thanks, Gary." Aidan lifted his eyebrow again. "Nice hair, by the way." Aidan grinned at me, spun around, and strode off.

"My name is Greg!" the man in question yelled at Aidan's back. He turned to me. "What's wrong with my hair?" He patted the short curls on top of his head and slid his hand down the longer hair in the back. "Rob Lowe wears his hair like this."

"Nothing's wrong with it. Aidan just likes to tease people."

"I don't think he's funny."

"Ooookay, no need to get worked up about it."

"I'm not worked up."

You could have fooled me. Time to change the subject. "Let me help you with those snacks."

I helped him drag a large box of sports equipment away from the snack cabinet and made a mental note to ask the janitor, Arnie, to move the box somewhere more appropriate.

Greg and I filled two boxes with bags of chips and two-liter sodas before heading to the parking lot. As we crossed the crowded lot to his car, he said, "I think I saw that guy last night."

"What guy?"

"The one who doesn't like my hair."

"Aidan? Where was he?"

"Right here in the parking lot. I arrived for the youth parents' meeting as the rehearsal was letting out. Aidan and another man were arguing by a truck over in the corner." He shifted his box into one arm and pointed to the far corner of the lot. "It was dark, and the other guy's face was turned away from me, but the conversation was heated."

"Hmm. Aidan does have a bit of a temper. That's one of the reasons he and Aunt Starla broke up." I dropped my box onto the backseat of Greg's car.

"The other guy pushed him, but he just stood there. Didn't hit him back or anything. Then he walked away. The other guy yelled something like, 'You watch your back.'"

"Sounds like guys being guys."

"I'm a guy, but I don't push and threaten other men for the fun of it. Your friend must have done something to deserve it."

"Knowing Aidan, he probably did. I'm not going to worry about it. He can take care of himself."

IT TOOK ME a half hour to wend my way back across the parking lot, because several people I hadn't seen in a while stopped me to chat. They were in no hurry to drive out to the reception, as the wedding party had to take pictures first.

I circled the corner to the front steps of the church as the photographer was attempting to herd the bridal party back into the building. I had missed the receiving line, but as I wasn't a guest, it didn't matter.

The photographer succeeded in her quest after a few minutes of cajoling. The Patrick family got their photos taken first, so Mr. and Mrs. Patrick could head over to the reception.

Bright sunlight streamed through the stained-glass windows on the west side of the sanctuary, creating colors and shadows that exasperated the photographer. The church's architects wouldn't have stopped to think about the effect of those west-facing windows on wedding photography. Sixty years earlier, weddings often weren't even held in churches, and cameras were few and far between.

The groom and groomsmen were photographed next, followed by the entire wedding party and then the women. The Burns family went last, and they took the longest by far. The bride's mother was very particular about where she wanted everyone to stand, and her grandchildren—the flower girl and ring bearer—weren't old enough to stay in one place for long, especially after having taken the full-group photos earlier.

After about twenty minutes of chaos, the bride realized they hadn't gotten a shot of the bride, groom, best man, and matron of honor. She called me over and asked me to make sure Aidan was still around to be in the final shots.

My scan of the sanctuary was futile. Several of the men were chatting with some bridesmaids near an open window in the back, but Aidan wasn't among them. A few of the groomsmen were lounging on the pews in various states of dishevelment. One was missing his jacket. Another had dispensed with his bow tie and cummerbund. A brown-haired man had even changed his shirt.

I approached the group. "Anyone seen Aidan?"

Two of the men glanced at each other in silent communication, but they said nothing. One of the women piped up, "I saw him head out that door after the group pictures." She pointed across the room to a door near the back that led to a hallway. "Then I saw a bridesmaid go through the same door after the women were done."

The woman's husband nudged her with his knee.

"What? I'm only saying what I saw. The woman is right over there." She used her head to point toward the mixed group at the back. "The redheaded one."

Also the prettiest one, I noted, when I spotted the woman standing a little off to the side of the others. Somehow, even though she was a redhead, she looked amazing in the pink bridesmaid dress. I headed over to her.

"Do you know where Aidan is?"

"Why in the world would I know where he is?" Her sharp response took me aback.

The man nearest her stepped over and wrapped his arm around her waist. "What's the problem here?" He was wearing a suit instead of a tux, so he wasn't part of the wedding party.

"I'm asking if anyone knows where Aidan is."

His eyes flashed with anger for a split second before he said, "I don't have any idea where that jerk is."

"Ooookay. I'm sorry to bother you about this, but I need help finding him so we can finish up the pictures."

One of the other men said, "I'm all yours. Tell me where to go."

I sent the helpful groomsman off to check the

bathrooms. A few seconds later, the mother of the bride bumped into me as she rushed down the aisle, husband in tow. I grabbed the arm of a pew to keep from falling, took a few deep breaths, and alerted the photographer that I was trying to track down Aidan.

I exited the sanctuary and walked down a hallway, peeking into each room I passed. As I approached the kitchen, the sound of running water reached my ears. Pink liquid was flowing out the door and spreading across the hallway.

"Aidan? Are you in there?" I gingerly stepped through the pooling water and through the kitchen doorway.

I tried to come to a stop as I took in the scene, but my foot slipped, my bad leg buckled, and I slid through the running water. I shrieked and windmilled my arms in a failed attempt to catch my balance.

Though I managed to grip the edge of the countertop as I teetered and pulled myself back up, I overcorrected and fell forward. My head glanced off the countertop edge, and the last thing my brain registered before everything went black was a white dress shirt closing in on my face.

TWO

WHEN I CAME TO, I didn't know if I'd been out for five seconds or five minutes. My face rested on someone's back, and when I moved my hand to my chest, my dress was soaking wet. Before I could collect my wits, voices reached me from the hallway.

"What in the blazes?" Three groomsmen skidded into the room as I lifted my head. They all came to a stop much more easily than I had done amidst all the water.

The shocked face of Marty James, local hardware store manager and the man directly in my line of vision, helped jolt me back to the situation at hand. I took stock of my position and let out a yelp. I clambered away from the man's body with as little grace as I had approached it. My feet slid through the water again, and I nearly knocked Marty over.

"I think we found Aidan," Marty said as he caught me.

Reality sank in, and I moaned as I collapsed back down into the water. Marty and one of Aidan's cousins—Zane, maybe—squatted next to me, but they both turned their bodies so they weren't facing Aidan.

The other guy, whom I didn't know, crossed to Aidan and felt for a pulse, though the act seemed unnecessary. He was dead. The bloody gash on the back of his head and the pink-tinged water still flowing across the floor was enough proof for me. I let the men help me stand, and I unsteadily spun away from Aidan. I didn't want to see him again, though I'd be replaying the scene in my mind for the rest of my life.

Marty grabbed a dish towel from the countertop and motioned to my face with it. I took it and gave myself a few good swipes. When I pulled it away, it was wet and covered not only with makeup but also some blood. I hoped the blood was from me and not Aidan, though I didn't think I was bleeding anywhere. I almost passed out again, and the guys held onto me until I was stable.

We all stood staring at each other for a few moments before my instincts started to kick in, as well as my knowledge of crime scenes, compliments of Agatha Christie, *Magnum, P.I.,* and *Murder, She Wrote.*

"Everyone, outside now," I said. "Don't touch anything else."

"Should we turn off the water?" guy-I-didn't-know asked.

"Grab a towel and use it to turn the tap off. Don't touch the knobs with your bare hands, and don't swipe the towel across the surface."

"Yes, ma'am."

"And grab some extra towels for me. I'm dripping."

The rest of us stepped out the door, and the sound of running water stopped. The third guy joined us in a few seconds and handed me some dish towels.

"Now what?" he asked as I dabbed my front and wiped my face some more. I squeezed the hem of my dress and more pink liquid trickled out.

I looked up to all three men staring at me expectantly. Me, the woman covered in bloody water. Me, the person who was here only to help with the wedding as needed. They were all pretending to be strong, but Zane was taking quick, shallow breaths, and Marty's face was much paler than usual. They needed someone to tell them what to do, and I would have no trouble doing it.

"Marty and ... Zane?"

He nodded in assent.

I pointed at the floor. "You stay here in the hall. Don't let anyone else go inside the kitchen until the police arrive." Zane closed his eyes for a moment before he nodded again, and my heart went out to him. I reached out and touched his arm.

"I know this is hard for you." I stepped back so I could see the other two guys as well. "It's difficult for all of you. But right now Aidan needs you. Can you do this for him?"

"We can," Marty said. "We'll do whatever we need to." He put a hand on Zane's shoulder and squeezed it.

I turned to the other guy. "I'm Beckett, by the way. You are ...?"

"Chuck."

I started down the hall and motioned for him to follow. "Come with me." I was almost certain Aidan's death wasn't an accident, and I was not going anywhere alone with a potential murderer in the building.

"Hold on," Chuck said and grasped my arm to stop me. "You're limping. Are you all right?"

"I always limp. Fell out of a tree when I was nine. It gives me an excellent excuse for my natural clumsiness." I started walking again. "We need to call 911. There's a phone in the kitchen, but we're not going back in there. We'll go to the office. I've got a key." I stopped short. "Wait a minute. Where's my purse?"

I wracked my brain trying to remember when I'd last seen it. "Oh yes, I stashed it in the armoire in the foyer." I pointed at Chuck. "You're much faster than me, so why don't you go grab it? I'll stay here." I was still in sight of Marty and Zane, so I felt safe staying where I was. I would have preferred to clean myself up a little more in the bathroom, but that could wait.

Chuck dashed off, and I called after him, "If you run into anyone, don't tell them what's happened!"

He gave me a thumbs-up as he headed toward the foyer. In less than a minute he was jogging back toward me with my purse. He thrust it into my hands, and I led him down the side hall to the office.

"I managed to avoid everybody," he said, "but through the open door I heard Shane ask if anyone had found Aidan yet. So we may have company soon."

As we walked, I dug around in the bottom of my purse in search of my keys. "Dang it, I've got too much junk in here." We reached the office door, and I dumped the entire contents of the bag onto the floor.

Chuck grabbed my wad of keys and passed them to me. I deftly picked out the correct key and let us into the office. Chuck picked up the phone receiver from Greg's desk and handed it to me as he dialed 911.

It rang once. "Cherry County 911, Donna speaking. How can I help you?"

I steeled myself for what I was about to say. "Hi Donna, this is Beckett Monahan, and—"

"Hey, Becky, how's it going?"

"I go by ... never mind. I've got a murder to report."

"Excuse me? Can you repeat that?" responded an incredulous Donna.

"You heard me. Aidan Patrick has been murdered. At least, it looks like murder. He's in the kitchen at First Community Church. Can you send the police over here?"

"Will do, Becky. They'll be with you in a jiffy. You sure he's dead?"

"Quite certain."

"Okay, I'll call the coroner too. Bye, now. You take care." As she hung up, she muttered, "Aidan Patrick murdered. If that don't beat all."

I turned to find Chuck on the floor gathering up the contents of my purse. He dumped a handful of Now and Laters back into the bag, while casting a smile my way. I grinned. What could I say? I've always had a weakness for fruity candy.

"Do we need to go outside so we can tell the police where to come?" he inquired as he handed over my bag.

"No, I told Donna he's in the kitchen. They'll know where to go. We'd better head back that way, because they'll be here soon. The police station is only a few blocks away. I should have enough time to stop by the bathroom for a minute to clean up, though."

I hurried back down the hallway, Chuck following in my wake. I stopped at the bathroom door and pivoted toward him. "Would you mind going in with me for a second to make sure nobody's in there?"

His forehead scrunched. "Why ... oh," his expression changed when he caught on, "sure. Wait here."

Chuck gave the room a once-over and deemed it safe for me to enter. My reflection in the mirror gave me a start and reminded me of what I had just experienced. My stomach quivered at the thought of Aidan's blood on me.

I leaned on the sink a few moments and took some deep breaths. Then I pushed the memory of the murder scene to the back of my mind and determined I would be strong and helpful for as long as I needed to be. I'd have time to fall apart later. I wiped my face with a wet paper towel and dabbed some more water from my dress. As I soaped and rinsed my hands, I noticed I had lost a pinky nail.

I tossed the paper towels into the trash can and stepped back into the hall, where Chuck was waiting for me. As we made the left turn toward the kitchen, Shane called out to us. He was coming from the direction of the sanctuary, and high-pitched shrieking sounded in the distance. We stopped. I wasn't sure what to do. How much did he know?

"Have you two seen Aidan?" Shane asked. "We need to finish up the pictures. Blair is about to have a coronary. Don't want to start off my marriage with a visit to the ER." He smiled, but then he furrowed his brow and touched my sleeve. "Becky? Why are you wet?"

Chuck and I shared a glance, and I gave him a nod. He was Shane's friend. I was only an acquaintance.

"Beckett, you go on ahead," Chuck said. He opened the closest door, which led to the youth room. He clapped a big hand on Shane's shoulder and tried to steer him through the doorway. "Shane, come in here with me for a second."

Shane tried to resist him. "We should be looking for Aidan!"

Chuck firmly, yet not unkindly, pushed Shane into the room. The door closed behind them as a siren began whining in the distance and slowly increased in volume. I headed on down the hall toward the kitchen.

Marty and Zane stood sentry in the hallway. I had no doubt they would stop anyone who came along. Past them two police officers appeared beyond the glass door at the end of the hallway. One of them pounded on it and the sentries both jumped. I skirted by them and tiptoed through the water toward the door while averting my gaze from the kitchen as I passed it.

The taller officer pounded on the door again a few seconds before I carefully pushed it open. If you shoved it open, the hinges would screech. "Darren Turley, you could see me. There was no need for that."

"You were taking your sweet time."

I pointed to my bad leg.

"Ah, yes. Sorry, Beckett."

"The door was unlocked anyway."

He ignored my comment and pushed past me as I held the door open. "The kitchen, you said?"

I pointed. "Yes, down—"

"On the left. I know. Wait." He stopped, turned on his heel, and looked me up and down. "What happened to you?"

I craned my neck to gaze up at him. He was almost a foot taller than me, and I wasn't very short. "I'm ... uh, I'm the one who found the ... uh, him. Aidan. I slipped in the water and fell on top of him. Hit my head on the way down and blacked out for I don't know how long."

Darren closed his eyes for a long second and then grabbed his walkie talkie. I couldn't understand all the numbers and other mumbo jumbo he and the person at the other end exchanged, but I gathered he was calling for an ambulance.

"I'm fine!" I protested. "At least physically. Mentally and emotionally, once this all sinks in, probably not so much."

"We still need to get you checked out." He pointed a finger at me. "Don't go anywhere." He strode down the hallway.

"Yes, sir."

The other officer held the door and motioned for me to go back inside. "After you, Becky."

I stepped in and stood aside as Officer Frank Nichols scurried down the hall after Darren. When Frank reached the kitchen doorway, he stood and took in the scene for a few seconds before entering.

Then it hit me. I didn't have to be in charge anymore. I put my back against the wall and slid down to the floor. My eyes closed of their own accord, and tears streamed down my face. I tried to think about anything but what was happening in the kitchen. Minutes later, the door screeched, my eyes flew open, and my hand jerked to my heart.

A paramedic kneeled beside me. It hadn't taken a rocket scientist to figure out I was the person they were there to see.

———

BY THE TIME the paramedics finished checking me over in the ambulance, a crowd had gathered in the parking lot. The group was a combination of curious passersby, church members, nearby business owners, and a few members of the wedding party. Some wedding guests had even come back from the reception site.

The scene was descending into chaos as everyone tried to determine what was happening. People were waiting to talk to me, since it was obvious I had been at least partly involved. The paramedics had shielded me from questions while I was in the ambulance, but once they released me, I was fair game.

The crowd pounced on me, everyone asking questions at once. One booming female voice carried over the rest, "Give the girl some space. Can't you tell she's been through the wringer?"

I wasn't sure how to feel about Veronica Coker's assessment of me—or calling me a girl—but for once I was thankful for my pastor's wife's take-charge personality.

"Thanks, Mrs. Coker." I had once made the mistake of calling her Veronica. It was not pretty. "I think I do need to sit down."

She took me by the arm and led me to one of the picnic tables at the edge of the parking lot. She sat angled toward me, leaned forward with her hands on her knees, and said, "Now tell us what's going on."

A small crowd had followed us and gathered around. I wasn't sure how much to tell them. The police wouldn't want me to give all the details, and I didn't want to recount them anyway. I'd rather never think about them again. Now that I *was* thinking about them—about him—tears filled my eyes.

To my astonishment, Veronica put an arm around me. "There, there."

I didn't realize anyone actually said that, but I was glad she wasn't pushing me.

"All we need is the basic facts."

Ah, so she was pushing me. I closed my eyes.

"She'll be giving you no facts at this time." Darren to the rescue. The Deputy Chief of Police held a hand out. "Come with me. I need to ask you a few questions."

I took his hand and allowed him to pull me to my feet as my eyes sent him a thank-you for getting me out of the situation. Sure, I'd still have to talk about it, but not with thirty people hanging on my every word.

The crowd parted for us as he led me back to the church building. We didn't go back into the door by the kitchen. Instead, he led me around to the entrance by the office on Main Street.

"We locked this door soon after we arrived. Do you have your keys?" Darren asked.

I fished them back out of my purse and let us in. Darren followed me into the office, and the space suddenly seemed much smaller. To be fair, it was compact.

The outer office held Greg's desk to the right inside the door, with my own desk to the left. Beyond my desk were twin windows overlooking Main Street.

Straight ahead, a wall separated the outer office from the pastor's inner office. Along that wall stood several bookshelves facing my desk, the door into the inner office, a tall metal file cabinet, a mimeograph machine, and a storage cabinet. Two chairs for visitors were pushed against the wall under the window between my desk and the bookshelves.

I walked past the desk attachment that held my typewriter and collapsed into my desk chair. Darren pulled up one of the other chairs to sit across from me. He whipped a small notebook out of his shirt pocket, flipped it open, and clicked his pen.

"Walk me through everything that happened from the minute you arrived here this morning."

Brrrrring!

I looked from Darren to the phone on my desk. "Do I answer?"

"Do you have one of those answering machines here?"

Brrrrring!

"No. Veronica says they're too impersonal."

"Yeah, but they're practical."

Brrrrring!

He waved his arm toward the phone. "You'd better answer it."

I picked up the receiver. "First Community Church. This is Beckett."

"Beckett Lee Monahan! I thought I was going to have a heart attack when I heard someone was murdered at First Comm. You couldn't think to call your mother and tell her it wasn't you?"

THREE

DARREN SHOT ME a wry smile. Mom was shouting, so he had heard every word. He circled his finger around to tell me to wrap it up.

"Mom, I'm fine. I'm talking to Darren now. I need to hang up."

She huffed into the phone. "Fine. Call me as soon as you finish. I mean it."

"Yes, ma'am."

"And tell Darren hello."

"Hello, Minda," the man in question called out.

"Bye, Mom. I promise I'll call later." I set the receiver back into its cradle.

"You'd better take that off the hook," Darren said. "Otherwise, we may never get a moment's peace. When we were in the kitchen it rang and rang."

I placed the receiver on the table next to the phone, but the dial tone annoyed me. I crossed the office to Greg's desk and took his phone off the hook instead. This was one time I was glad the deacon board had voted against getting a second phone line.

I settled back into place at my desk, took a deep breath, and began my story. When I finished, Darren put his pen down and gave me an assessing look.

"What?"

"How do I know *you* didn't murder him?"

I sputtered. "Are you kidding me? Why would I kill Aidan? I don't have anything against him."

"Maybe not, but I don't know that for sure." He swept his hand toward my dress. "His blood is all over your clothes."

"Because I fell on him—*after* the fact! I also have an alibi. I was in the sanctuary the entire time they were taking photos."

"Were you? The whole time? Can anybody confirm that?"

"At least fifty people were in there!"

"Exactly. Enough that nobody will remember if one particular person was there the whole time unless they were in every single photo or taking the photos."

I shifted in my seat when I realized I had left the sanctuary to use the restroom.

"You're acting suspicious," he observed. "What are you not telling me?"

I had never been great at keeping secrets—even my own.

"I remembered I did leave the sanctuary."

He picked up his pen again. "When, and how long were you gone?"

"While the bride was taking pictures with the bridesmaids. I couldn't have been gone more than a couple minutes."

"Did anyone see you?"

"I don't remember seeing anyone else."

"Hmm." He clicked his pen a few times. "Can you tell me what order the photos were taken in? That may help us figure out whose alibis hold up."

Darren took notes as I recalled the order. He then tapped his pen on the notebook and said, "Aidan was in the sanctuary for the full-group photos. Then the women went. How many minutes do you think that took?"

"Ten minutes? Fifteen?"

He scribbled more notes. "Then the Burns family. How long did that take?"

"Forever. The kids were all over the place. At least twenty minutes passed before Blair sent me off to track down Aidan."

"How long did you look for Aidan before the three groomsmen found you on top of his body in the kitchen?"

I shivered at the memory. "I was only gone about a minute before I found him, but I don't know how long

I was out before the guys found me. I doubt it was long, though. Blair was getting antsy to finish the photos, so she would have sent them looking within minutes."

He scribbled in the notebook. "Doing the math here ... Aidan was potentially out of the sanctuary for about a half hour before you found him, and then another few minutes until the guys found you."

"That sounds right."

"The only people we can say for sure were in the sanctuary the entire time are the bride and the photographer?"

"I think so."

"That doesn't narrow down the suspect pool too much."

My eyes opened wide at "suspect pool." Someone in this town—probably someone I knew—had murdered Aidan.

"Hold on," I said. "Wouldn't the murderer have blood on their own clothes? Can that help you cross everyone still in the church off the list?"

"They might have changed their clothes."

"Not the wedding party."

"True. It's also true that Aidan's injuries might have occurred in a way that the murderer didn't get a drop of blood on them."

I flung my arms out. "Blood was everywhere!"

"It seemed to be everywhere because of the water. There wasn't a whole lot of it."

"Why was the water running and overflowing?"

"Someone—likely either Aidan or the killer—had turned on the water, but a pitcher was blocking the drain, so eventually the sink overflowed."

I thought for a moment and tried to stick my pinky nail between my teeth, but something wasn't right. I jerked my hand out of my mouth and placed it palm down on the desk.

"Something wrong?" Darren sounded like he knew the answer.

"I lost a nail." I touched one of the remaining fingernails. "They were brand new."

Darren gestured to the mess of papers, books, and bulletins covering my desk and typewriter and said, "You sure it's not here somewhere?"

I narrowed my eyes at him. "I haven't even been at this desk today until now."

He pulled a small, clear bag out of his pocket and set it in front of me. "Is this the nail?"

"Where did you find that?"

I reached for the bag, but he snatched it away before I could touch it.

"Next to Aidan's body. Care to explain how you lost

a nail, if all you were doing is looking for Aidan?"

I sputtered. "You know I didn't do it! I grabbed the edge of the counter when I slipped. That must be when it came off."

He looked into my eyes for a moment and then gave a slight nod. He wrote something in his notebook.

"You should re-enact the water thing," I said. "Test it and find out how long it takes to overflow and spread all the way to the hallway. That may give you a better idea of the timing. I can help you do it!"

He snapped the notebook shut and stuck it, his pen, and my fingernail in his shirt pocket. "Leave the police work to us, Beckett. Thanks for talking with me." He stood, gave me a nod, and turned to leave.

I pushed to my feet. "Wait! Aren't you going to tell me how he died? I think I'm owed at least that much, seeing as I was up close and personal with him and his blood."

Darren swiveled toward me. "We're keeping that information confidential at the moment."

"Ooookay, then." I was annoyed, but I had read enough murder mysteries that I understood why. "Do I already know anything else you're keeping confidential?"

"I don't think so." He paused. "Would you be able to keep it confidential even if there were?"

I chuckled. "How do you know me so well? We haven't spent that much time around each other."

"I'm a policeman. It's what I do." He tilted his head to the side. "And maybe Starla has mentioned it a time or two." Darren had been dating Aunt Starla for a few months.

"Oh my gosh! Do you think Aunt Star knows what happened?"

He stared at me until I caught on.

"This is Cherry Hill," I said. "Everybody knows by now."

"Yes, and I'm guessing your mother has talked to her. I also used the kitchen phone to call Starla and ask her to come pick you up. I would guess she's waiting outside."

Interesting that he had her phone number memorized.

"Now that I think about it," he said, "I should escort you to her car. I doubt the crowd has thinned."

"Thanks, I'd appreciate that."

"And if you want to leave your own car keys with me, we'll make sure it gets home to you."

I handed over the wad of keys, and we made our way to the outside door. Though nobody had been at that entrance when we came in, a crowd had now gathered. Darren pushed open the door to multiple voices asking us what was going on.

"Not now, folks," Darren said. "Beckett needs to go home and rest, and Frank and I have a lot more people to interview inside the church." He lifted his hand and waved someone over. The crowd parted to reveal my aunt racing toward me.

Aunt Star and Darren flanked me and swept me through the onlookers and into my aunt's brand-new, candy-apple-red Camaro Z28. I hoped I wouldn't get any blood on the upholstery. She didn't pump me for any information as we drove the few blocks home.

My mother was waiting in the driveway when we arrived. As soon as I hauled myself out of my aunt's low-sitting car, Mom wrapped me in her arms. When we pulled apart, she failed to conceal her look of horror when she realized the dampness my clothes had transferred to hers may be more than water. I thanked her for coming, but I also sent her home, since what I needed most at the time was a shower. I was certain she would be taking one too.

I stepped into the garage, and Aunt Star closed the overhead door behind me.

She said, "Why don't you slip your dress off out here? I'll take it to the dry cleaner's later."

I was already pulling the ruined dress over my head. "Don't worry about cleaning it. I never want to see this thing again."

Aunt Star held out a paper grocery bag, and I pushed the dress into it. She stuck it into the metal trash can as I opened the door into the house. I crossed through the kitchen, climbed the stairs, and made a beeline for the bathroom across the hall from my room.

———

A HALF HOUR later I shuffled into the kitchen wearing my comfiest robe, with my hair wrapped in a towel.

Aunt Star was sitting at the table with a half-eaten Twinkie and a large, nearly empty wine glass in front of her. These were both signs she was very upset, because she rarely indulged in any unhealthy food or drink. Yet she appeared unflustered and had changed into a peach wind suit. With her short, blonde, feathered hair, she resembled Princess Diana.

I sat across from her at the glass-topped table.

She jumped up. "Coke or something stronger?"

"Coke, please, and a few crackers. I'm hungry, but I'm also feeling nauseous."

"That's understandable."

I leaned my head on my hand while she poured me a Coke and pulled a box of Ritz crackers out of the pantry. She set them on my placemat and returned to her seat.

"Do you feel like talking about it?" She took a sip of wine.

Brrrrring!

Aunt Star stood and grabbed the kitchen phone from the wall by the refrigerator. "Yes?"

She mouthed to me, "Your mother."

I waved my hands to tell her I wasn't prepared to talk to Mom yet.

She returned to her chair and said into the phone, "Yes, she's cleaned up. ... She's not quite ready to talk about it." She winked at me. "Yes, I'll make sure she calls you later."

Aunt Star is Mom's much younger sister. In fact, she's as close to my age as to Mom's. She's ten years older than me and ten years younger than Mom. My uncle Ernie is halfway between the two of them. Mom and Aunt Star have always had a bit of a rocky relationship, which wasn't helped when I moved in with my aunt instead of my parents after moving back to Cherry Hill a couple years ago. Mom felt betrayed, but she was mad at her sister about it instead of me.

Aunt Star twirled the phone cord around her pointer finger as my mother gave her an earful about something. "Yeah, we'll talk about that another time. Bye." She pushed back to her feet to hang the phone up.

"What are you going to talk about another time?" I hated that I was so nosy, but I couldn't help it.

"I might as well tell you." She returned to her seat and took a sip of wine before continuing. "I saw Aidan a few times over the past month."

I leaned toward her. "What do you mean, you saw Aidan?"

"We went out."

"What?" I sat up straight. "How did I not know about this?"

"We met during the day while you were at work."

"That explains why I didn't notice you were gone, but why didn't you tell me?" I pouted a bit.

"Because you wouldn't approve." She took a giant bite of Twinkie.

"Uh-huh. Because you're seeing Darren too."

She swallowed before pronouncing, "Darren and I are not officially dating. We're perfectly free to go out with other people."

"Does he know that?"

"We haven't talked about it." She tapped her fingernails on the table, avoiding my eyes.

"I doubt he's on the same page about that. Do you think he has heard about you and Aidan?" I asked. That might make *him* a suspect!

"I don't know." She tilted her head. "You didn't."

I rolled my eyes. "There's a good chance he did. He knows everything that goes on in this town."

"So do you." She gulped her wine and took a deep breath. "That's not all. The last time Aidan and I met, we got into a fight."

Brrrrring!

FOUR

AUNT STAR PICKED UP the phone again. The strident voice on the other end started in before she could get a greeting out. She rolled her eyes and finally got a word in.

"I'm sorry, Edna, but I'm not going to let you talk to her today." Edna Thorn was the editor of *The Cherry Hill Standard,* our weekly newspaper. "You don't go to print tomorrow, so this can wait. Try her tomorrow *after* church. I can't make any promises about what she'll tell you. ... Mm-hm." Another eye roll. "Bye."

She hung up the phone, took it back off the hook, and picked up her wine glass. "Let's take this into the living room."

I followed her with my glass of Coke and settled into a corner of the light pink couch. Aunt Star sat across from me in a pink-and-baby-blue-striped easy chair and tucked her legs under her.

She recently redecorated our—technically her—living room in pastels and light-colored wood, as that was the new trend. I liked bright, bold colors myself. This was her house, though, and the furniture was high quality and comfortable, so I couldn't complain. I also liked it better than the previous 70s decor of dark wood along with olive green and rust orange *everything*.

"What did you and Aidan fight about?"

Aunt Star looked at the ceiling to keep tears from falling. "I'd rather not talk about it."

I knew not to push her when she didn't want to talk. And I had only seen her cry a handful of times in my life, so I didn't want to upset her any further.

"Let's talk about you instead," she said. "How are you feeling?"

"It all seems so surreal since I left the church." I sat up straight. "I was supposed to lock up the building after the wedding! I need to go back over there."

"I'm sure someone has taken care of it. The Cokers were in the parking lot."

I had already forgotten my interaction with Veronica Coker. Her husband, Harold, was the pastor of First Community Church, and she was the self-appointed overseer of all things First Comm. She would make sure everything was in order at the church. I imagined she had tried to start cleaning the crime scene before the police were finished.

I relaxed back into the couch and propped my feet on the coffee table. "I bet Darren and Frank will be there the rest of the day. They'll have to talk to everybody who was at the church."

My mind ran through all the people that entailed, which didn't include Aidan's parents. "Aidan's poor family! What was supposed to be a great day has turned into a total tragedy. I wonder how his parents found out. I really hope they didn't hear about it through the grapevine."

Aunt Star said, "Veronica had run home from the reception to grab a sweater, and she saw the police cars. So of course she found out what was going on. When she discovered the police were going to send an officer to give Aidan's parents the news, she told the officer to tell Harold instead, who would tell Mr. and Mrs. Patrick. She thought it would be better for them to find out from their pastor than from a policeman. As much as I hate to admit it, she was right."

"Where did you hear all that?"

"Callie called me during her break while you were upstairs."

Callie Collister was Aunt Star's lifelong best friend, and she was a waitress at The Checkered Cloth diner—otherwise known as "The Check"—across the street from the church. She always had an ear on every table and an eye on Main Street. I didn't know *how* Callie had learned the details of how Aidan's parents were informed of his death, but her information would be mostly accurate.

"Apparently you know more about what's going on than I do," I said, "even though I was the one who was lying face-first on his dead body."

I shuddered and tried to push the memory away. Replaying it in my mind wasn't going to help anyone. I needed something to focus my energy on—some way to help. I sat up with purpose. "I'm going to find the person who did this to Aidan if it's the last thing I do. I need to do it for his parents and for Shane."

My aunt leaned toward me. "Becks, your love of helping people and solving problems is Cherry Hill's worst kept secret, but this one might be a bit beyond you. Solving crimes is the police's job. Plus, a murderer is running around town, and you don't want to find yourself on their bad side."

"I'll be discreet," I said.

"You wouldn't know discreet if it hit you on the nose. Case in point ..." she swept her hand up and down, referencing my current clothing choices: hot pink slippers, an orange-and-yellow-checked fuzzy robe, and a kelly green towel wrapped around my hair.

I sighed. "You're right, but I have to do this. I'll be

careful, I promise."

"You'd better be. I'll help you in any way I can. Aidan may have been a pain in the rear a lot of the time, but I did care about him. And his parents are such amazing people. They deserve to know what happened to him. I have no doubt in Darren's abilities, especially with his police academy training and his experience in St. Louis, but Frank and the other Cherry Hill cops have never even dreamed of having to solve a murder. I don't think we've had one in the entire county in my whole life."

"Then we're going to solve this murder!" I thrust my pointer finger in the air as I said it.

Ding-dong!

"That'll be Trixie." Aunt Star got up to answer the door. "I called her while you were in the shower and asked her to come by. I have to go show a house. Why somebody wants to go house shopping at 7:00 on a Saturday night is beyond me, but I'm not going to argue with a potential customer." She turned her head to me as she reached the door. "I only argue with them once a contract is signed and they want to do something ridiculous."

I was laughing as my best friend stepped into the living room.

"You must be doing fine if you're laughing." Trixie

frowned as she crossed the room to sit by me. I almost laughed again as I observed her trying to decide if she was going to hug me. Trixie isn't a touchy-feely person. After a few seconds, she patted me on the leg.

"Aunt Star said something funny," I explained.

My aunt said, "She's in a better state of mind than earlier because she found a way to help. That always energizes her."

Trixie nodded. "How are you going to help? Bake cookies for the Patricks?"

"Nooo," I said. "We," I pointed at Aunt Star and myself, "are going to find the killer."

"You two," Trixie repeated my pointing, "are going to solve Aidan's murder?"

I was a little offended by the incredulousness in her voice.

"Why not?" I retorted. "We're smart women."

"I'm sorry," Trixie said. "You are smart, but you're not trained to do this. The police are."

"Correction," Aunt Star said, as she put on her jacket and gathered up her purse and keys. "Darren is trained to solve a murder. The rest of the Mayberry police force is not. We thought we'd help them out a little. I think Becks has some great skills we can use to find out who killed Aidan. She can convince anyone to tell her anything, and I have all kinds of connections. I've bought or sold a house for anyone who's anyone in this county."

Aunt Star had sure changed her tune. She had always been protective of me, and that was coming to the forefront.

"I keep putting my foot in it," Trixie said. "Are you sure you're all right?" she asked and tentatively touched my leg again. "I can't imagine what it's like to find a dead body."

"Not *a* body, but Aidan's body. And not only find it but fall on it."

"Excuse me, what?!"

"Sorry to interrupt at this exciting moment," Aunt Star said, "but I need to go."

"Be careful," I said. "Are you coming home right after?"

"I guess," she said. "I was supposed to meet Darren for a drink at The Blue Barn, but I don't think he'll be able to make it."

"Nope. See you later."

"Don't forget to call your mother," she said as she swept through the doorway into the kitchen. A few seconds later, the door leading into the garage slammed.

AFTER TRIXIE LEFT, I changed into my pajamas and released my curls from the towel. Then I called Mom and gave her all the details—more than I wanted to share, but she had her ways of getting details out of me.

Once she was satisfied I'd told her everything, she said, "I'm guessing your aunt hasn't fed you, so your dad's bringing over a lasagna. He should arrive any minute."

My mother thought a lasagna would fix anything. You'd think she was Italian, but all four of her grandparents had immigrated from England in the early 1900s. Dad was one hundred percent Irish, which had been a source of contention between all their parents. None of that explained the lasagna. Yet it was her thing, so I was getting a lasagna whether I wanted it or not. I wasn't hungry, but arguing with her wouldn't accomplish anything.

Ding-dong!

"He's here, Mom. Talk to you later. Love you."

I ushered my dad inside as Aunt Star pulled into the driveway. He had no idea what to do with the lasagna pan, so I took it from him, and he followed me into the kitchen. I set it down on the stove and he gave me a bear hug.

"How's my girl?" He put his hands on my shoulders

and looked me in the eye.

"I don't fully know. This has been a long day."

"I bet you're tired."

"Very. I'm going to bed soon, I think."

Aunt Star entered the kitchen from the garage. "Not yet. Darren and Frank are here. They brought your car back." She dropped my keys on the counter. "They're also coming in. Frank said they've got a few questions and he'd come to the front door with Darren. Not sure why he was being so formal."

Dad's eyebrows drew together. "They need to leave my girl alone. She didn't do anything wrong."

"Stay calm, Dad. I didn't do anything wrong, and they know that. They just need more information."

Ding-dong!

"I'll get out of your hair then," Dad said as he hugged me again and kissed my forehead. "I'll see you at church tomorrow."

He opened the front door to reveal the two officers on the porch. They all stood in silence for a few moments. Dad was facing the other way, but I was familiar with the "don't you dare mess with my daughter" look he was undoubtedly giving Darren and Frank. He finally stepped past them and headed to his car.

I motioned for the two men to enter and thanked

them for bringing my car home. Frank was his usual jovial self. The man simply couldn't help smiling, even during a murder investigation. Darren, on the other hand, had a face like thunder.

"Sorry to bother you, ladies," Frank said, "but we have some questions for Starla."

"Starla!" I exclaimed. "Why do you need to talk to her? I'm the one who was there."

Aunt Star wasn't fazed. "I was expecting this, but not so soon. Come on into the kitchen."

I sat opposite Frank, while Aunt Star slipped into the chair across from Darren.

Darren placed a hand on the table in front of me and I turned to him.

"You don't need to be here. In fact, you really shouldn't be here since we're not questioning you. And you look like you're ready for bed."

I glanced down at the Betty Boop pajamas I had forgotten I was wearing, and my face turned red. At least they covered everything.

"She can stay," Aunt Star said. "I have nothing to hide from her."

I gave her a sideways glance. She had certainly been hiding something from me, and that "something" was almost certainly why the police were here. I returned my gaze to Darren, who was assessing me. He hadn't missed my look. I needed to work on my poker face if I was going to be a secret investigator. I tried to appear calm, but I feared it wasn't working.

"Starla," Frank began, "it has come to our attention you've been dating Aidan Patrick. Is that true?"

Aunt Star paused for a moment before speaking. "I wouldn't say we were dating, but we did go out a few times, yes."

"Let me get this straight," Darren said through clenched teeth. "You weren't dating, but you went out on dates?"

"Yes, we did."

"Where did you go and what did you do on these dates?" he spat out.

She cocked a brow at him. "Is that relevant to the investigation?"

Frank shot Darren a look. "Not necessarily," Frank said. "The main thing we need to talk to you about is a fight the two of you had the other day."

How had they even heard about that? Aidan must have talked about their interactions more than she had.

"What about it?" she asked.

"When did it happen, and what was it about?" Darren couldn't look her in the eye.

"It was on Tuesday. We met in Taylorville *for lunch,*" she said with a pointed look at Darren. "He's building a house over there."

Aidan was a building contractor and was in high demand in Cherry County.

My aunt continued, "When he walked me to my car afterward, he tried to convince me to be his date to Shane's wedding. He'd been hounding me about it for weeks. I was surprised he even wanted a date, because I figured he'd want to be free to spend the evening with a bridesmaid. I refused. I didn't want everyone to think we were a couple." She leaned toward Darren and waited until he looked at her. "Because we weren't."

"How did that turn into a fight, exactly?" His tone was a little friendlier than it had been a few minutes earlier.

"Aidan was livid that I wouldn't say yes. He has— had—a bit of a temper when he didn't get his way. He said a few choice words to me, and I gave him some right back. Then he stormed off to his truck and peeled out. I hadn't talked to him since."

Darren leaned forward. "Did he get physical with you?"

"I'm assuming you're asking if he hit me and not the other kind of 'getting physical,' because that would be an inappropriate question. No, he didn't. He wouldn't. He's a yeller, not a hitter. Can you imagine me putting up with a man who hit me?"

Darren sat back in his chair and his scowl turned to a grin. "No, I can't."

"Any more questions?" Aunt Star asked.

"No." Darren flipped his notebook shut, but he didn't stand to leave.

I jumped up. "Would you guys like something to drink or eat? I bet you didn't even eat dinner. My dad brought us a pan of lasagna. You're welcome to some of it."

"That would be great, if it's not too much trouble," Darren said, and Frank nodded his head.

"Becks, you sit," Aunt Starla said. "I'll serve. Do you feel like eating now?"

I plopped back down in my chair. "I do. Bring on the lasagna!"

We made small talk to reset the mood in the room, and then I asked, "Did you finish up at the church? Do you have to interview more people tonight?"

Frank started to answer, but Darren cut him off. "We can't talk about the investigation." He pointed at me. "Technically, you're still a suspect."

FIVE

AUNT STAR BANGED A plate of lasagna down in front of Darren. Luckily, the dish was from our new Corelle set and didn't shatter. "Darren Turley, you know this child didn't do it."

I bristled a bit at the "child," but I appreciated the sentiment.

She put her hands on her hips. "We don't need all the details, and you don't need to be rude. She's trying to make conversation. Do you want us to sit here in silence?"

Darren sighed and shook his head.

Frank said, "I guess we can tell you gals anything anyone else might already have heard. Nothing wrong with that, right?"

He turned to Darren, who grudgingly nodded.

"Did you interview everybody at church?" I inquired. "A lot of people were still there."

Darren swallowed and wiped his mouth with the back of his hand. "We called in the whole force to help, so we got through initial interviews with everybody at the church and sent them home. We got their phone numbers so we can follow up. Chief Dover was at the reception, so he did some interviews there with a few people who arrived late enough to potentially be suspects."

He took another bite and Aunt Star handed him a napkin.

I tapped my finger on my chin. "Anyone else in town who wasn't at the reception could be a suspect. All the church doors were unlocked. Somebody might have slipped in without being seen or without anyone being suspicious about their presence."

"Right," Frank agreed, "but not many people had a reason to kill Aidan. Darren here taught me you gotta have three things to make somebody a suspect: means, motive, and ... what was the third word?" He looked at Darren.

"Opportunity," Darren filled in around a bite of lasagna.

Frank waved his fork at me. "Yep, opportunity. Lots of people had opportunity, but most don't have a motive."

"Beckett doesn't have a motive! So why is she still a suspect?" Aunt Star slapped the table. "I had more of a motive than she did."

"Ah, so you admit you *did* have a motive," Darren

said.

"No, I did not. He was upset with me. I wasn't upset with him."

Darren flipped his notebook back open. "You said, and I quote, 'He said a few choice words to me, and I gave him some right back.'"

"A few choice words about his character—that I later regretted saying, by the way—not about wanting to kill him. You know I didn't do it."

"He does," Frank said. "He was just mad you went out with somebody else." Frank flinched. "Ouch!" He frowned at Darren. "What did you go and do that for?"

Darren sighed. I don't think he's capable of blushing, but if so, he would have been.

"Does anybody have a real motive?" Aunt Star asked.

"We've got a few we're looking into," Frank said. "One of the groomsmen—ouch!" He turned to Darren. "Why in the world do you keep kicking me? Keep your feet to yourself."

Darren swallowed his last bite of lasagna, put his fork on his plate, and shoved his chair back. "We need to get on these feet and head back to the station. Lots of reports to write up tonight. Thank you, ladies, for the food. Let's go, Frank."

Frank shoveled the rest of his lasagna into his mouth

and stood. "Ladies, that was delicious. Becky, tell your mama we enjoyed her lasagna."

I didn't even bother to correct him about my name. It would be no use with Frank.

———

WHEN I ARRIVED at church the next morning, the parking lot was abuzz, even though I arrived thirty minutes before Sunday school started, as usual.

"Beckett!" a woman's voice called out from the church's back door the second I stepped out of my car. Suzanne LaHaye, First Comm's volunteer worship leader, was waving me over. I should have known she'd be the first to corner me.

My car door creaked as I slammed it shut. I pushed on the frame to make sure it was closed all the way. My beige, four-door 1968 Ford Torino was a hand-me-down from my grandma Pearl. It was not pretty and made a lot of strange noises, but it ran. Considering I couldn't afford another one on my church secretary's salary, I was stuck with it.

I smoothed down the skirt of my royal blue dress and set out across the lot. Several people tried to stop me to chat, and I waved them off, but they all fell into step beside me. I guess they figured they'd hear my story sooner or later if they stayed close enough.

Suzanne held the door open, and we all trooped through. I held my gaze straight ahead when we passed the kitchen. My entourage peppered me with questions all the way to the office. I answered them as succinctly and generally as possible, without giving away any details I didn't think the police would want me to tell.

I pushed open the office door and was assaulted by the smell of mimeograph fluid. Somebody must have needed some copies before I arrived. I stopped and turned to my adoring crowd before stepping into the office.

"Anyone who needs my help related to Sunday school or today's church service is welcome to come in. Otherwise, I'll see you later."

Most of the crowd dispersed, but Suzanne bustled in and squeezed her frame into one of the office chairs. She patted her hair, as if the excessively hair-sprayed tight curls could possibly have moved out of place.

"Now," she drawled, "tell me what *really* happened."

"What do you mean?" I asked as I dropped into my chair.

"Of course you couldn't tell them anything," she said with a wave of her hand toward the door, "but you can tell me everything." She pretended to lock her mouth and throw away the key. I almost laughed at the gesture and at the idea of Suzanne keeping anything to herself.

"I've told you everything I can."

"The police have to have an idea of who did it, though, right?" she probed.

"I can't comment on that."

Suzanne huffed, and I shrugged.

"I never thought you'd be like that."

"Like what?" I demanded.

"All secretive."

"This is a murder investigation. We're not talking about a drunken fight in a parking lot."

Speaking of fights in parking lots, Greg had mentioned something about Aidan arguing with another man after the rehearsal. The other man could well be the groomsman Frank talked about. I glanced over at Greg's desk.

"Have you seen Greg yet this morning?" I asked.

"No, I haven't." She braced her hands on the arms of her chair. "I can tell I'm not going to get anything from you this morning, so I'm heading to the choir room. I expected better of you, Becky Monahan." She maneuvered herself out of the chair and pointed at my desk. "And clean up this mess. It's a disgrace." While the door closed behind her, she left a parting shot.

"You should know more than a few people think your aunt did it."

I shook a fist at the closed door and then slumped in my chair. I had to prove those people wrong, whoever they were.

I extricated a notebook from the mess on my desk, opened to a fresh page, and printed "SUSPECTS" at the top. I bit my pinky nail while I considered who to add to the list. The nail was now safe, since I'd removed the nine remaining press-on nails last night and added clear polish.

The first person I added to the list was the unnamed groomsman. If the police were interested in him, he had a motive. He also had the opportunity, as the groomsmen were finished with pictures early. I wasn't sure about the means, because I still didn't know exactly how Aidan had died. I needed to find that out. I flipped to another page and wrote: "How did he die?"

My thoughts drifted to the red-haired bridesmaid who had been seen leaving the sanctuary after Aidan did. She and her date both had an issue with Aidan.

Piano music drifted into the room. Choir practice was starting, which reminded me I had a job to do that didn't involve catching murderers. I turned to the "Suspects" page, added the bridesmaid and her date to it, closed the notebook, and shoved it into my purse.

———

I HAD SCHEDULED myself to work in the nursery during the church service, for which I was grateful. The kids were already in the room from Sunday school, so I didn't have to interact with any of their parents before church. The other volunteer was a sweet older lady who wouldn't badger me. The biggest advantage, though, was getting to snuggle babies for an hour.

After church was a different story. As each parent came to retrieve their child, they asked questions or gave me looks of pity or even suspicion. I wasn't sure which option was worse. One woman even asked me if it was true Aunt Starla had been dating Aidan. I told her in no uncertain terms it was none of her business. After she stalked away, I realized my response probably made her even more suspicious.

Finally, the last child was gone, and my mother appeared in the doorway as I was putting toys away.

"Opal, would you mind finishing up here while I take my daughter to lunch?" Mom asked the other volunteer.

Opal, bless her, readily agreed.

Mom steered me through the church, across the street, and into our usual booth at The Check where

Dad was waiting for us. In less than a minute, Callie appeared with our drinks, without us even having to order them. I took a sip of my Coke.

She patted me on the shoulder, "How you doing, hon? Hanging in there?"

"I'm hanging in there when it comes to me, but a lot of people think Aunt Star killed Aidan."

"Noooo," my mother said. "How can anyone believe that of her? She's an upstanding citizen of this community!" Mom and Aunt Star might have problems with each other privately, but publicly, they were staunch supporters of each other. And no matter where we were, Mom would never believe her baby sister had killed anyone.

"I heard that rumor this morning," Callie said. "And I immediately shut it down."

"Thanks," I said. "We all appreciate it."

"Of course I'm going to stick up for her. She's done it plenty for me," Callie gestured toward the chalkboard on the wall. "Special's on the board, or do y'all want your usuals?"

The special was tacos and rice. Mexican food was a rarity at The Check, so I jumped on it.

"I'll take my usual burger and fries," Dad said. He was a creature of habit.

Mom ordered chicken-fried steak and mashed

potatoes, and Callie threaded her way to the kitchen between the free-standing tables covered with red-and-white-checked tablecloths.

A car backfired on Main Street, and we all turned toward the window beside our booth. The car was speeding away, but was that Chuck walking down the sidewalk across the street? He turned his head toward me, which confirmed it. I gave a small wave, but he put his head down and kept walking. I frowned at the window.

"Who were you waving at?" Mom asked. "I don't recognize that man."

"One of the guys who helped me yesterday—a groomsman."

"He doesn't seem too friendly," Dad observed.

"He must not have recognized me."

The bell on the diner door jingled behind me, and Dad waved at the newcomer. "Greg, come join us if you're not meeting anyone," he called out.

"I had planned on getting a burger to go," Greg said as he approached our table, "but since you asked ..."

I scooted over to make space for the youth pastor. He squeezed my arm as he settled into his spot. Within seconds, Callie arrived with a glass of iced tea for him. He ordered the special and she headed off again.

Greg angled his body toward me as much as

possible in the tight booth. "I didn't get a chance to talk to you at church about what happened. I tried to call you last night, but the line was busy."

I filled him in on the general details. Then I asked, "How did things go with the boys?"

"We never got around to watching the movie. The kids were all too upset about what had happened at church. Cory Hankins was torn up about it. He said his dad and Aidan have been best friends their whole lives, but they fell out about something last month. It was bad enough that Aidan didn't go to Cory's last few basketball games."

Dad said, "Steve Hankins is one of the most mild-mannered men in Cherry County. I can't imagine he would ever have a falling out with anyone."

"Me either." I nudged Greg. "Tell me more about the argument you saw in the church parking lot Friday night—the one with Aidan and some other guy. Did you hear anything you didn't mention to me yesterday? Can you describe the man?"

Mom cut in, "Aidan had a fight with yet another person? What was happening with that man? He's never been my favorite person—I didn't like the way he treated Starla all those years ago—but this seems excessive."

Before Greg had time to answer my questions,

Callie arrived with our food. How she had the ability to juggle four plates at once was beyond me.

She set our plates in front of us and then cocked one hand on a hip. "I overheard you talking about Cory Hankins. I don't know what happened between Aidan and Steve, but it's not right that Aidan cut Cory out of his life. They've always been close. Cory even calls him 'Uncle Aidan.'"

"Yeah, that's what he called Aidan last night," Greg said.

Callie continued, "And Cory's been having some trouble at school. I think he almost got suspended last week after a scuffle in the locker room." She angled her elbow toward Greg. "You'd probably know about that, since you're at the high school a lot."

Greg was only a part-time pastor at First Comm, so he was also a substitute teacher at the junior high and high school two or three days a week. He had only been in Cherry Hill for a few months, but he had integrated right in to our tight-knit community.

"Yes," Greg said, "he's gotten into trouble a few times over the past month or so, which people say isn't typical for him. That's part of the reason I asked the guys over to my house last night. I wanted to give them a place to come where they'd stay out of trouble and maybe talk about some of the stuff that had been happening at school."

"Cory has a good head on his shoulders. Keep trying to spend time with him." Callie strolled off to take care of another table.

I opened my mouth to repeat my questions to Greg, but before I could get a word out the diner bell jingled again, and the entire place went silent. I turned and craned my neck so I could see the door. Blair Burns Patrick was standing in the entryway. Her hair was a mess, and her eyes were wild. "You!" she shouted and pointed at me.

SIX

ME? WHAT HAD I done to Blair?

She marched toward me, still pointing. My dad and Greg both leapt to their feet and blocked her path.

"Ma'am," Dad said, "what seems to be the problem here?"

Blair pushed past him, put her palms on the table, and leaned toward me. I scrunched into the corner of the booth.

"You ruined my wedding!"

Greg put a hand on her arm, but she shook him off.

"She did no such thing," my mother said. "You need to settle down, missy."

Blair swung her gaze to Mom. "You stay out of this, old lady."

That was the exact wrong thing to say to my mother. She rose out of her seat—as far as she could in a booth—and got right into Blair's face. "I. Am. Not. An. Old. Lady. My daughter did not ruin your wedding, but you're sure as heck ruining our Sunday lunch. Shame on you."

Blair stared at her for a few seconds before her face crumpled and she slid to the floor in a sobbing heap, knocking over two cups as she went.

The men seemed unsure of how to deal with this change of events. I recovered from my initial shock, and my heart went out to the newlywed.

I kneeled next to Blair and wrapped my arms around her as she howled. Once again, I was on a wet floor in a strange situation. At least this time everyone was alive.

"Here, honey." Callie slipped an arm around Blair. "Let's get you up off the ground."

Callie and Dad worked together to help Blair stand and slide into the booth. Mom wasn't any too pleased to have Blair now sitting by her. She moved all the way over against the wall, likely as much to keep herself dry as anything else.

I sat sideways in the booth so I could dry my legs with some napkins. Callie pulled a chair up to the end of our table, and the men sat at the empty table next to us and gave us all wary looks. Another waitress brought a mop to clean up the puddle on the floor.

Since I was still preoccupied with patting my legs dry, Callie took charge of the conversation. "Now, miss ... Blair, right?"

Blair nodded and sniffled. I shoved some napkins

across the table to her.

Callie leaned toward Blair. "What's the problem here, honey? And don't tell us Beckett ruined your wedding, because she absolutely did not."

"Then Aidan ruined my wedding!" She stomped her foot, though not with much emphasis.

"Did he, though?" Callie asked. "I'm thinking the person who murdered Aidan is the real wedding ruiner."

"He probably did something to deserve it," Blair said. "He can be a complete jerk when he feels like it."

"I won't argue with you on the second part." Callie and Mom were united in their dislike of Aidan. "But I can't imagine he deserved to be killed. A punch in the nose? Yes. Death? No."

My mother bobbed her head up and down. She would have relished watching someone punch Aidan, but she would not want him to be murdered.

"I should be on my honeymoon right now, and my wedding was ruuuined," Blair wailed.

"Yes, it was. No one is denying that," Mom handed Blair even more napkins. Even she could sympathize with a ruined wedding, regardless of the reason.

I turned to face Blair. "We understand you're upset. It was a horrible thing to happen at any time, and especially during your wedding, but none of us were at fault. Let's put our energy into helping find the person who did this. We need to do that for Aidan and for your husband. Right?"

Blair begrudgingly nodded.

"Now," I said, "can you think of anything— *anything*—that happened with Aidan that might help us figure out who did this?"

"Beckett," my mother said with narrowed eyes, "there is no 'us' in this investigation. There's the police. Don't you get involved. We don't need you getting killed too."

"Amen," my dad muttered from the next table.

I needed to keep my involvement even more off the radar than I had thought, but I wasn't going to sit quietly and not pull any information out of Blair.

"Mom, I'm only trying to help Blair remember. Then we can go tell the police what she said, if anything seems relevant."

"I talked to the police yesterday," Blair said. "There's not much more to say."

"Yes, but yesterday you were in shock. You might remember something else now that you've had time to process." Apparently not enough time, but I wasn't about to say that. "Can you think of anyone who might want to hurt Aidan?"

"Welllll ..."

"Spit it out," Mom said.

Blair glared at her, but she did as she was told. "My bridesmaid Tonya—you know, the red-headed one?" she glanced at me.

I nodded.

"Tonya had a huge crush on Aidan. I think something happened between them at our engagement party, but I'm not sure what. I told her to stay away from him, partly because Aidan can't be trusted with women, but mostly because Tonya's engaged. Her fiancé Nathan was at the wedding, and I think he figured out something had been going on between Tonya and Aidan. I don't like Nathan much, but I don't think he'd kill Aidan."

The bell on the door jingled again.

"We'll let the police be the judges of that," Callie said.

"Be the judges of what?" Darren asked as he approached our table.

He'd had no trouble overhearing Callie from the doorway, as the other customers had been silent since Blair had made her entrance. He nodded at Dad and Greg before standing at the end of our table with his hands on his belt.

"What's happening here? We got a call about a

disturbance."

"Everything's fine," I said. "Blair was upset, but we've worked it out."

Blair gave me a slight smile.

I continued, "And she told us something very interesting. Might give you a suspect or two."

Darren sighed. "I told you to stay out of the investigation."

I silently stared at him.

"But thank you," he finally said. I nodded.

"Mrs. Patrick," he said, "I'd like you to come down to the station with me and tell me what you told these ladies."

Blair was silent a few seconds until she realized he was talking to her. She slowly got to her feet.

Darren and Blair hadn't been gone thirty seconds when Edna Thorn, the newspaper editor, slipped into the empty spot Blair had left at our table.

"I figured y'all would be here after church, as usual," Edna said.

"Edna," my mother started in, "don't you dare pester Beckett about what happened yesterday."

I held my hands up. "It's okay, Mom. I don't mind talking to her."

My primary goal was finding out what Edna knew. We soon discovered she had no information we didn't.

I gave her the bare-bones facts of what had happened, and I made sure not to let any information slip that I had found out from others. She wasn't happy with my lack of details, but I didn't need to be quoted in the paper saying things the police wouldn't want me to share.

———

WHEN I GOT HOME, Aunt Star was curled up in her chair watching *Flashdance* for the eighty-seventh time. She watched it when she wanted to forget about the world for a while. This was not the moment to tell her some of our fellow townspeople suspected her of Aidan's murder.

I also needed a distraction, so I made myself comfortable on the couch and watched the last half hour with her. As the tape rewound, I sang the chorus of "Maniac."

Unfortunately, the lyrics brought me back to reality. Aidan's killer was certainly a maniac, and not the kind the song was talking about.

"I think you're going to have to work on Darren," I said to my aunt. "He's not going to tell me anything except that I should stay out of the investigation."

"Did you talk to him again?"

I told her about the interaction with Blair at The Check.

"Interesting," she said. "That certainly gives Tonya's fiancé a motive, and possibly Tonya too. The story doesn't make a lot of sense to me, though. Say what you will about Aidan, but he would never knowingly be with an engaged woman."

"Maybe he didn't know."

She chewed her cheek while she thought for a moment. "Maybe not. And that might be where the problem lay. What if, after the party, Aidan found out Tonya was engaged? He knew she would be at the wedding, so he would need a buffer. That might be why he was so insistent on taking me with him."

"Yes! And maybe she tried something at the rehearsal or wedding, and he rejected her." I jabbed the air with my finger. "That'd give her a motive too. Somebody did say they saw her leave the sanctuary after he did." We were naturals at this detecting thing. "We need to tell the police."

"They may know," she said, "but we should tell them in case they don't."

"I don't think it should be me. Darren is already irritated with me, but he'd listen to you."

"He'd better," she said. "I do think I need to be our main contact with Darren while we investigate. You talk to Frank. I have no doubt you can wheedle information out of him, as long as Darren isn't around."

"You should set up a date with Darren."

"I should, but not tomorrow, because that's my favorite girl's birthday!"

I had completely forgotten about my birthday. "Oh, yeah! Dinner at Mom and Dad's."

"How about drinks afterward at The Blue Barn?" she asked.

"Sure. You can invite Darren to that. I don't mind. And I'll ask Trixie and Scott, though I don't know if they could both come with such short notice. They'd have to find a babysitter." But if they did, I'd be the fifth wheel. That wouldn't be fun, especially on my birthday. "And maybe I'll invite Greg."

"Good for you! You need to get back out there."

I hadn't been on a date in almost two years, since I broke up with my fiancé and moved back to Cherry Hill. I had thought Walter was the one, obviously, since I'd said yes when he popped the question. But in the end it hadn't worked out. Walter hadn't been happy when I ended it. Neither was I, but it had to be done.

"It wouldn't be a date. Greg's a good guy, but I'm not interested in him that way. His life doesn't seem very stable. He moves around a lot."

"You're not marrying the guy. You're simply inviting

him to your birthday party."

"You have a point. I'll call him and Trixie. I'll let you call Darren."

Greg was able to come, and Trixie said her parents would be happy to watch Krystal and Victor, so she and Scott were both in.

Aunt Star was in her bedroom folding laundry when I went to tell her the phone was free. I also needed to warn her about the rumors involving her.

"Phone is free." I stood there chewing my lip.

She eyed me. "What? I can tell you have something to say."

"There might be some people in town who think you did it."

"'Did it' as in killed Aidan?"

I nodded.

She kept folding towels. "They'll be proven wrong soon enough."

I couldn't believe how calmly she took the news that people in our town thought she might be a killer.

"You don't care." I said this more as a statement than a question.

"It's not a great feeling when you realize people think you could be a murderer, but I know I'm not, so I'm not going to worry about it. I don't care what people think." She carried a stack of bath towels into her bathroom.

How could she not care? I cared!

From the bathroom, she yelled, "Before you tell me you care, I realize that, and I appreciate it. Instead of spending your energy worrying about rumors, keep working to find the killer."

I sighed. "Okay, I'll try." I was going to work overtime trying to solve this murder, if only to get people off Aunt Star's case.

A cabinet door slammed, and she reappeared.

"By the way," I said, "I learned something else today about Aidan." I helped her fold the rest of her laundry as I told her about Aidan's falling out with Steve Hankins and the effect it had on Cory.

"Aidan hadn't told me about that. I'll make sure to mention it to Darren. He and Steve play basketball together on Saturday mornings, so he may have already heard."

"Look at you, knowing Darren's schedule." I added a folded washcloth to the towering stack. Why did one person need so many washcloths?

"Aidan played with them too," she said. "Though maybe not since whatever happened with Steve."

"You were playing with fire, weren't you? Did you not think they'd find out you were also going out with the other one?"

"Oh, Aidan knew. Since I explained Darren and I aren't exclusive, he was fine with it."

"So you were only keeping it a secret from Darren."

"And you," she said.

I grabbed her pillow and flung it at her.

———

THE NEXT MORNING, I awakened to the sound of Glenn Frey singing "The Heat Is On." I slapped the snooze button on my clock radio to give myself another nine minutes of sleep.

A storm during the night had woken me several times. I was in no mood to get up yet, but the fast beat of the music had gotten my heart rate up enough that sleep wasn't coming back.

I lay there staring at the ceiling until my nine minutes were up and Madonna's voice singing "Crazy for You" filled my bedroom. That song was more of a morning speed. I sang along in my head until it was over and then crawled out of bed.

As I searched my closet for the new outfit I intended to wear to work, the top of the hour hit, when Y107's morning deejay gave a rundown of the morning's news. "This just in: There has been an arrest in the murder of Aidan Patrick in Cherry Hill."

SEVEN

I LEANED OUT OF the closet and stared at the radio, as if the deejay were sitting there talking to me in the flesh.

"Police have not yet released the name of the suspect. We will update you as we have more news. In today's weather, a cold front has arrived ..."

I raced down the hall and flung open Aunt Star's bedroom door so hard it ricocheted back toward me and hit my shoulder. I hissed at the slight pain. The sounds startled my aunt awake, and she sat straight up.

"Becks? What's happened?" she said drowsily, but with concern in her voice.

"Somebody's been arrested!"

Aunt Star rubbed her eyes. "Who? And stop yelling. I'm right here."

"I don't know!" I lowered my voice. "They didn't say."

"Who didn't say?"

"The deejay. He said he'd keep us posted. He won't keep us posted. That guy doesn't care what happens in Cherry Hill." I pounded my fist on her dresser for emphasis.

"Beckett, calm down." She was fully awake now if she was calling me Beckett.

"Can you call Darren and find out what's happening?"

She ran her fingers through her hair at the mention of Darren's name. "No, I cannot call the police station and ask who they arrested."

She was right. They wouldn't tell her, but I needed to know. Was it the bridesmaid Tonya or her fiancé? Or Steve Hankins? Or maybe the groomsman I never did find out about?

"Happy birthday, by the way."

Yet again, I had forgotten about my birthday.

"Thanks." I paused. "What are we going to do?"

She pointed at me. "You are going to go to work, and I am going to work, and we will go about our day."

"But—"

"This is Cherry Hill. We'll hear all the details by noon."

———

I HAD ALL THE details well before noon. The hubbub

from the church office greeted me as I entered the outside door. I stepped into the office to find Veronica in a state. Our pastor's wife is never in a state. Yet there she was.

Veronica's short, black hair was pointing in all directions, and she was speaking in a much higher register than usual. However, the most shocking aspect was seeing her diminutive frame wrapped in a silk robe that didn't completely cover her lacy pajamas. The outfit was completed with a pair of unlaced tennis shoes.

"This can't be happening!" she kept saying over and over. Her husband repeated, "There, there," and gently moved her into one of the visitors' chairs as I dropped my purse on my desk. Greg watched her with wide eyes. He had no idea what to do with a hysterical woman, and especially this one. Someone needed to take control of this situation—whatever it was.

"What *is* happening?" I asked and pulled the other chair around in front of Veronica to talk to her at her level. I reached out and patted her shaking hand. She grasped my hand and gripped it so tightly I couldn't help but cringe.

"Suzanne ... was arrested ... for Aidan's murder!" Veronica broke down in sobs.

You could have knocked me over with a cotton ball.

"Suzanne? No way!"

"Yes ... way!"

This was a turn of events I never would have predicted. How would our fifty-five-year-old worship leader have managed to kill a man more than a foot taller and fifteen years younger than her? I couldn't imagine it. And why? What motive would Suzanne have to kill Aidan?

"But why?" I asked as I extricated my hand from hers. "I mean, why would she kill him?"

Veronica sobbed. I patted her knee and turned to her husband.

He raised his palms in confusion. "She raced in here about a minute before you arrived, and we haven't gotten anything coherent out of her."

This was an unprecedented situation. Veronica not having complete control of herself was something I had never witnessed. Not being fully dressed and made up at 8:30 a.m. was another thing I had never expected of her. Not that I cared, but normally *she* would care.

"Veronica," I said loudly and took her head between my hands. "You need to focus. Tell us what happened."

She blinked a few times and took a deep breath. I dropped my hands.

"F-frank called me. From the police station. He said he couldn't tell me anything except they had arrested Suzanne, and he asked if I would tell Jacqui. He thought she would take it better from me."

Jacqui was Suzanne's daughter who had moved back to Cherry Hill from California a few months earlier after an acrimonious divorce. She had a son in second or third grade who had come to church with Suzanne a time or two.

Based on our current situation, the police shouldn't have told Veronica the news either. Frank couldn't have imagined Veronica would respond like this, though.

"Did you call Jacqui?" I asked.

"N-no. I couldn't. Can you do it?" she pleaded.

This situation had done a number on Veronica if she was asking me to do something instead of telling me to do it.

"Sure."

I had no idea what Jacqui's phone number was, and she was too new to be in the phone book, so I called the operator. Within a minute, I was connected.

Jacqui took the news much more calmly than Veronica had. She told me her car wasn't running, and she hadn't been able to take it to the shop yet, so I agreed to pick her up and take her to the police station.

I was more than happy to help, and I'd surely get firsthand information about what was happening.

Greg offered to answer the phone while I was away. I wasn't sure he knew what he was getting into, because as soon as word got out about Suzanne, the church phone would start ringing off the hook.

Before I rushed out, Pastor Coker said, "Beckett, please don't tell anyone about ..." He swept his hand toward his wife, who was staring off into space.

"I won't. You can count on me!" Nobody would believe the story if I did tell it.

I rushed out to my car and followed the directions Jacqui had given me to her house. When I pulled up, I recognized it as one of Suzanne's rental houses. Her husband had died several years earlier and had left her with a hefty savings account and a giant life insurance policy. She had chosen to invest her money in rentals, which Aunt Star acknowledged had paid off for her. Not that she needed any more money.

Jacqui raced out of the house as I grabbed several paperbacks, a crumpled Dairy Queen bag, and a sweater from the passenger seat and tossed them in the back. She yanked the door open and plopped in.

"How much do you know?" she asked.

"Nothing except your mother has been arrested for Aidan Patrick's murder. I can't imagine why. Can you?"

Jacqui pursed her lips and stared out the windshield. "No," she said tersely.

Obviously, the answer was yes, but she wasn't going to give me a straight answer. I tried to make small talk, but after a few one-word answers from her, I gave up.

I observed her out of the corner of my eye as I navigated the streets of Cherry Hill. Her straight black hair was pulled back with a fancy red barrette. She was dressed in tight stonewashed jeans and a blue-and-red-striped sweater that showed more cleavage than any sweater I'd ever seen in real life. She wasn't wearing a coat, even though the temperature had dropped quite a bit over the weekend.

She was amazingly put together at 8:15 a.m. for a person who lived with an eight-year-old and didn't have a job. She continued to stare straight ahead. I didn't break the silence again.

When we arrived at the police station, Jacqui didn't ask me to go with her, but I trailed behind her as she marched in. She started to walk right past the receptionist's desk, but Barbara Young was having none of that. The receptionist rolled her chair over to block the doorway to "the pit," the open area where all the officers' desks were located.

"Can I help you, miss?" she asked. She looked past

Jacqui and nodded at me. "Becky."

I nodded back. This was yet another time I wasn't going to correct my name.

Jacqui retorted, "You know who I am, Barbara, and you know why I'm here. Don't act like you don't."

"My apologies, Jacqui."

Barbara was most decidedly not sorry. She was usually at least a little bit personable, but Aidan was her cousin. She was not going to be friendly to anyone who might have been connected to his death.

"Are you going to let me back there or not?" Jacqui demanded.

"Deputy Chief Turley is leading the investigation. While I run back to check if he's available, you can sit over there." Barbara pointed to one of the metal folding chairs lined against the wood-paneled wall of the lobby.

They had a stare down, but Barbara continued pointing until Jacqui gave in and sat. I took a seat two chairs down from her. I was a little scared of her at this point. In fact, I'd always been a little in awe of her. She was several years older than me, so I hadn't known her well at all when we were growing up. Their family had money, as her dad was one of the three lawyers in Cherry Hill. Jacqui was also very popular—cheerleader, prom queen, and student council president.

Barbara returned and very formally said, "Deputy Chief Turley will see you now."

Darren stepped into the doorway and stopped there. He most certainly did that as a power play, since he practically filled the entire doorway.

Jacqui wasn't impressed.

"Darren." Jacqui stood.

"Jacqui," he replied in an identical tone of voice.

My eyes bounced from one to the other as they faced off for a moment. Eventually, Jacqui moved toward him, and he motioned her through the doorway. Instead of following her, he turned to me and crossed his arms.

"Why are you here?"

"I was her ride."

He nodded. "You don't have to stay. We can make sure she gets home."

I wasn't going anywhere. "I'll stay. She might not want to be seen returning home in a cop car."

"Suit yourself." He jerked his head toward Barbara. "There's no point in trying to pry information out of her. She's a vault."

"A truer word has never been said," stated the woman in question.

Darren gave me one last hard look and stepped into the pit. Jacqui followed him to his office in the back.

"Is Frank here?" I asked Barbara.

"Nope. Don't you even try to weasel anything out of him if you do see him, Becky."

"Me? I would never."

We both knew I was lying.

They didn't have any copies of *Cosmopolitan* or even *Redbook* on the rickety side table next to my chair, so I picked up a six-month-old copy of *Popular Mechanics* to peruse as I waited. I was engrossed in an article about TVs small enough to fit in the palm of your hand—imagine!—when the ringing phone pulled my attention back to the police station.

Barbara's conversation with the unknown caller wasn't about Aidan's murder, so I lost interest. I turned my attention toward the outside door as Frank stepped out of his patrol car in the parking lot.

I stood, whispered, "I'll be right back. Stretching my legs," to Barbara, and stepped outside. I immediately regretted my choice not to grab my coat. I moved away and to the side of the glass door out of Barbara's line of sight and waved Frank over. He adjusted his route and headed toward me with his bowlegged gait.

"Hey there, Becky. What are you doing over here? Shouldn't you be at work?"

He stopped in front of me, stuck his thumbs into his

belt loops, and rocked back onto his heels.

"I brought Jacqui over," I explained. "Her car's acting up."

"Ah. It's the darndest thing, isn't it?"

"Her car acting up?" I rubbed my arms in a vain attempt to keep warm.

"Nope. Her mama being our top suspect in Aidan's murder."

"I don't understand why Suzanne would kill him. She's not the kindest person, but I can't imagine her murdering someone. Can you?"

"You know I can't tell you that." He scratched his chin.

I had to get him to tell me something—anything. I put on my best puppy-dog face and spoke softly, "Veronica is very upset about it. I'd like to be able to tell her at least something about what's going on. You gave her a huge shock when you called her this morning." I hated that I was manipulating Frank, but I needed information.

"I'm sorry I upset Veronica. I was trying to do the right thing."

"I know you were. Don't worry about it." I rubbed my goose-pimpled arms some more.

"Let's talk about this inside. You're cold."

Frank tried to take me by the elbow and escort me,

but I stood firm. Once Barbara was in earshot, I would get nothing out of Frank.

"I'm fine. Just enjoying the fresh air."

He didn't believe me, since my teeth were chattering, but he didn't question my response. I leaned toward him as a reminder I was waiting for some information to pass on to Veronica.

Frank finally said, "I guess I can tell you it has something to do with her daughter."

"Jacqui? What's she got to do with it?"

"I can't say anything else. I'd better head inside." He took a step toward the door.

I grabbed his arm. "Can you at least tell me how Aidan died?"

Frank sighed and turned back to me. "We don't have the autopsy report back. Should come in later today."

"You must have a guess, though. You're a smart man."

He stood taller at my compliment, but he didn't respond.

"Come on, I'm going to find out eventually. If you tell me something, at least I won't be speculating and potentially spreading wrong information." I gave him my sunniest smile.

"I guess you did see him, so you deserve to know. We think he was bashed in the back of the head with a hard object, which may or may not have killed him. Then when he fell, he hit the front of his head on the counter edge. That's where most of the blood came from."

I put a hand on his arm. "Thanks for telling me. I appreciate it."

Frank gave me a nod and entered the station. I waited a minute before returning so Barbara wouldn't be suspicious.

EIGHT

FRANK'S INFORMATION WASN'T all that helpful. The killer could be anyone with enough height and strength to swing a hard object high enough to whack Aidan on the back of the head.

I did wonder what type of object the person might have used. The murder must have been a spur-of-the-moment thing. Nobody could have predicted Aidan would be in the kitchen when he was, so the murder weapon had to have been something in the room. Maybe a rolling pin? Or a skillet?

The questions jogged a memory of the box of sports equipment Greg and I had moved away from the snack cabinet. I closed my eyes to try to picture the moment. A baseball bat had been sticking out of the box. I wondered if the bat was still there. I made a mental note to check the kitchen when I returned to the church.

After fifteen silent minutes in the police station lobby, I was getting a little antsy. *Popular Mechanics* had lost my interest. Barbara had gone into the pit, and

I was all alone. I decided it might not be a bad idea to see if anything on Barbara's desk could give me a clue.

I craned my neck to make sure nobody in the pit was looking my way, and I stood. Since I needed to like I was wandering, I crossed to the door and looked out for a few moments. Then I acted engrossed in the wall calendar sponsored by a local insurance agent, but the pictures of covered bridges didn't hold my attention for long. I finally let the pages fall and, after ensuring nobody was paying attention to me, I sidled over to the desk.

Several file folders, papers, and notepads were in plain view, but I couldn't spot anything related to the case. I inspected everything again more closely and something caught my eye. A small yellow note pad had a top blank page, but the top right corner of a previous page was still attached to the pad, and part of the letters "ick" were visible.

I needed the blank page so I could use the trick I learned in elementary school where you rub the side of a pencil across a piece of paper to reveal what had been written on the page above it. Could I tear the blank sheet out without anyone hearing? I had to try it. I grabbed the page and tore it off as slowly and quietly as possible.

"Becky, what do you think you're doing?"

I spun around so quickly my bad leg buckled. Thankfully I caught myself on the edge of the desk and didn't end up on the floor. Barbara watched me with crossed arms.

"Um, I needed to write a note. Can I use this paper?"

"I guess so, since you seem to have already taken it ... without asking first ... in a *police station*."

Now Barbara expected me to write a note, but I couldn't very well write it on the piece I had torn out. I also needed to leave so I could discover what the note said.

"The note was going to tell you I need to get back to work. If Jacqui needs a ride home, give me a call." I folded the paper neatly and stuck it in my purse. I prayed Barbara wouldn't ask me why I still needed it.

"Suit yourself," Barbara said as she slipped back behind her desk. "We'll call if we need you."

She would definitely not call.

———

I ENTERED THE church building through the door nearest the kitchen. I stopped before I got to the open kitchen doorway, closed my eyes, and took a deep breath. The day before, I had avoided looking in. I would have to walk into the kitchen again sometime, though, and I needed to try to find out what the murder weapon was. Not that the knowledge would necessarily help me, but you never knew what information might come in handy.

I opened my eyes, squared my shoulders, and stepped into the room. For some reason, I hadn't expected the same view I'd always had when entering the kitchen. The island, which held the sink, was completely clear. The other countertops held a few small appliances and containers, though not as many as usual. The box of sports equipment was gone. I would need to find it, but first I had to search the kitchen for potential weapons.

The room was full of hard objects: thick wooden cutting boards, rolling pins, pots and pans, and giant coffee cans. The weapon must have been something easy for the killer to grab. They wouldn't have opened a cabinet or drawer in search of something to knock Aidan over the head with.

I closed my eyes to picture the kitchen as it usually was, and more specifically the way it looked when I made the lemonade after the wedding. Usually, a large, open canister stood next to the stoves, which were inside the door to the left. The canister held a variety of spoons, spatulas, whisks, and, I was pretty sure, a rolling pin. The container wasn't there, so I opened cabinets until I found it. No rolling pin.

That could mean many things. Perhaps it hadn't been there in the first place, or the police might have bagged it as evidence. The killer may have taken it with them or even hid it somewhere else in the building.

I closed my eyes again, but I couldn't think of anything else the killer could have grabbed, other than the bat. I checked the closet in the kitchen, but the box of sports equipment wasn't in there. Then I investigated the adjoining fellowship hall, but it wasn't there either.

Next, I crossed to the preschool classroom across the hall from the kitchen. The room appeared to be in its normal state, with its miniature tables and chairs, but I flipped on the lights and stepped inside to make sure. The door to the small storage closet was slightly open. I crossed to it and opened the door.

Bingo! The box had been shoved into the tiny space, which was why the door couldn't shut all the way. A few other boxes had been placed on top of it. I turned on the closet light and removed the smaller boxes. Though no bat was sticking out of the box, I dug down to the bottom just in case.

It didn't make sense that the bat wasn't there. The

police might have taken it, but why was the box in the closet? Had the police even seen it? I couldn't imagine why anyone would think this closet was a good spot for this particular box unless they were trying to hide it.

I smacked myself on the forehead when I realized I had touched the door handle to the room and the closet, as well as the light switches, boxes, and almost everything in the big box. If the murderer had moved the box here, I had undoubtedly ruined fingerprint evidence.

The police needed to know what I had found. Or did they? I hadn't found anything concrete—only a box without a potential murder weapon in it. They might think I was silly if I said something. I'd need to think about it before mentioning anything to Darren or Frank. Unless I had some compelling evidence to share, Darren didn't need to know I was trying to solve this murder.

When I returned to the church office, Veronica was fully clothed and had fixed her hair and put her makeup on. I checked my watch. She had completely transformed in less than an hour. Impressive. "Mrs. Coker, you doing okay now?"

"Of course," she said with a sniff. "Why wouldn't I be?"

We were apparently pretending nothing out of the ordinary had happened this morning. Fine by me. I was still a little unsettled by it.

I considered whether I should mention anything about my conversation with Frank or the missing baseball bat and rolling pin, but I concluded nobody in the room needed to hear about that yet.

Instead of answering Veronica's question, I whipped the piece of yellow paper out of my purse and waved it for all to see—"all" being Veronica, Pastor Coker, Greg, and, I finally noticed, my aunt.

"Aunt Star, what are you doing here?"

"I heard about Suzanne and wanted to check on you."

More likely she wanted the latest news and knew we'd be the ones to provide it.

"What's with the paper?" Greg asked.

"Evidence," I said as I scooted around my desk and dropped my purse on the floor. I cleared a space on my desk and set the paper down. Everyone gathered around.

"It's blank," Veronica said. "How is this evidence?"

"Hold on a minute."

The only pencil in my desk drawer was worn down to a nub, but I needed it sharp, so I stuck it in the electric sharpener on my desk. Pastor Coker jumped when the grating started. Remarkably, everyone stayed silent.

I removed the pencil and carefully rubbed the side of the lead across the paper. Words started to appear. Heads drew closer. Greg put his hand on my shoulder as he leaned in. I stilled.

"Do you mind?" I asked.

They all straightened back up, and Greg removed his hand. I stretched out my arm and resumed my task.

"That's enough," Aunt Star said. "Stop with the dramatics and read it to us."

I swept the pencil across the surface a few more times, picked up the paper, and cleared my throat. "It says, 'Shane Patrick, Suzanne LaHaye, important info,' and a local phone number."

"Give me that." Veronica snatched the page from my hands, as if she might discern something from it that I couldn't.

She slapped the paper back down on my desk and returned to her seat.

"That doesn't tell us anything."

"I disagree," I said and paused for her reaction to my statement. She was silent, so I continued, "It tells us Shane had something to do with Suzanne's arrest."

"But what?" Pastor Coker asked.

We all considered in silence for a few moments.

Greg stepped back and sat on his desk.

I said, "I would guess he's the one who turned her in."

"That makes the most sense," Aunt Star said, "but what did he tell the police? And how did he know it?"

"We're going to find out!" Veronica declared.

Everyone turned toward her.

"We are?" Pastor Coker asked her.

"Of course we are, Hare-Bear." I tried not to snicker at the nickname. Veronica didn't seem to realize she'd said it.

She continued, "We all know Suzanne could never have done this. We have to clear her name. Is everyone on board?" She looked at each of us in turn, and we all nodded our assent. Heaven help anyone who would dare say no.

I was more irritated by Veronica's take-charge attitude than usual. Aunt Star and I were the ones who were going to get to the bottom of this murder, though that objective was different than clearing Suzanne's name. I also didn't want this whole group to know we were trying to solve the case.

I was surprised Aunt Star hadn't challenged Veronica, though. My aunt had pursed her lips and crossed her arms in front of her chest, but she hadn't argued with the pastor's wife.

Veronica clapped her hands once, and my head snapped up in response.

"Harold," she said, "you go visit Aidan's parents. You'll want to find out how they're holding up. Make sure you ask when his body will be released after the autopsy, so we can plan the funeral dinner. Also see what you can learn about what Shane told the police."

Her husband nodded in obedience.

"Beckett and Starla, why don't you go over to The Check and find out if any of the waitresses have heard anything that would be useful. I'm sure they have."

Going to the diner was what I would have decided to do next, so it worked for me. I grabbed my coat, and Aunt Star put her hand on the doorknob in anticipation of her escape.

Veronica turned to Greg. "You stay here and man the phones. People will be calling to find out what we know. Instead, ask what *they* know. See if anyone knows what Suzanne was doing during the time of the murder. She wasn't at the wedding, so she might have been anywhere."

Greg hopped off his desk and sat in his chair, ready to do her bidding.

"And I," she said, "will visit all the businesses within sight of the church. I'm going to make sure nobody out there thinks they saw Suzanne anywhere near First Comm on Saturday afternoon. Everyone meet back here at noon." She clapped twice. "Okay, people, let's do this."

Veronica slipped on her coat, and Aunt Star opened the door for her to sail through.

NINE

"I DO *NOT* LIKE it when that woman is in charge," Aunt Star pronounced as we settled into a booth at The Check.

"Me either," I responded, "but you have to admit she does a good job of running things."

"Eh," she said noncommittally. "She's confident in her abilities. And she's very sure Suzanne isn't the killer." She paused. "I can't see Suzanne doing it, either. Chances are the killer *is* someone we know and would never suspect, though, so we can't fully discount her."

I tapped my fingernails on the tabletop as I pondered what I had learned about solving crimes from my vast experience as a mystery reader and TV watcher. After no more than ten seconds, Aunt Star grabbed my hands to still them.

I jerked my hands from her grasp and said, "It's going to be hard to prove Suzanne didn't do it. Innocence is often hard to prove unless the person has a rock-solid alibi. But what we *can* do is prove someone else did it. That would confirm Suzanne's innocence." I pointed at Aunt Star. "It will also prove you didn't do it, in case people still think the worst of you."

Aunt Star rolled her eyes. She still didn't care if people thought she was a cold-blooded killer.

"You're saying we should leave proving Suzanne's innocence to Veronica, and instead stick with our mission of finding out who *did* kill Aidan?" Aunt Star asked.

"Exactly."

I reached into my purse, pulled out my notebook, and opened to the page titled "Suspects."

Aunt Star raised her eyebrows and said, "Aren't you prepared?"

I sighed. People often underestimated me, and normally I let it go. Not this time. I wasn't letting another person try to lord it over me, and on my birthday of all days. I had given Veronica a pass due to her state of mind earlier in the morning, though I probably would have anyway. Veronica was scary, but Aunt Star was pushing it.

"Yes, as a matter of fact, I am prepared. I am a professional woman, and I am perfectly capable of being responsible."

Her eyes opened wide. She hadn't expected my

outburst, and for good reason.

"I'm sorry, Becks. Truly. You're totally capable. Tell me about your list."

She sipped her coffee while I described the three suspects: the still unnamed groomsman, the red-haired bridesmaid Tonya, and her fiancé Nathan.

I added, "I'm guessing one of these two men is who Greg saw arguing with Aidan in the parking lot after the rehearsal."

"But you don't know for sure?" Aunt Star asked.

"Nope. Greg couldn't see the guy's face."

"Then you'd better add 'parking lot guy' to the list. There were a lot of men in the wedding party, plus any partners of the women who might have been there. This could very well be a different man than the two you've written down."

I added him to my list.

"What about Steve Hankins? And Cory?" My aunt reminded me about the teen and his dad who had been on the outs with Aidan.

"You can mark Steve off your list," Callie said as she stopped by to refill Aunt Star's coffee. "Turns out he went to visit his uncle at the hospital in Columbia on Saturday afternoon."

We stared at her.

"What? I asked around. You act like you've never

met me."

Another customer called for Callie, but before she walked away, she said, "I'll be back. There's more."

"Hmm," I said. "I won't add Steve to the list. What about Cory?"

Aunt Star and I looked at each other regretfully for a few seconds before I slowly wrote his name. "He had motive, and he's almost a grown man. He was big enough to have done it."

"I can't believe he would have, though," my aunt said, "but you're right. We can't count him out."

"Oh! I forgot to tell you what else I found out this morning."

I told my aunt what Frank had said about the murder weapon and explained that the rolling pin and baseball bat were both missing.

She said, "Sounds like one of those was probably the weapon. Did you tell the police about the bat?"

"No. What am I going to tell them? Somebody moved a box and maybe took a bat? I also don't want to get Frank in trouble."

"Good point," she said. "We need to keep him talking. That won't happen if Darren finds out he's feeding us information."

Callie returned, coffeepot still in hand. She set the pot on the table and slid into the booth next to Aunt

Star. She leaned in, and we followed her lead.

She spoke quietly so surrounding customers couldn't overhear. "I'm sure you want to know what I know about Suzanne. I'll get to that, but first, somebody said one of the groomsmen was very upset with Aidan. Something to do with the groomsman's sister." She cut her eyes toward Aunt Star. "Sorry."

"Don't be," Aunt Star said. "I was well acquainted with his exploits. The man got around."

Yet she was dating him again. What had she been thinking, especially when she had Darren?

"The guy's name is Chuck," Callie said. "That's all I know."

"Chuck!" I exclaimed.

Callie gave me a wide-eyed glare. "Why do you think I was being quiet? Now everybody's listening."

"Oops." I whispered, "Sorry."

She stood and said, "I need to take care of the other customers and give them time to forget to listen to us ... or to leave. I'll be back to find out what you know about this Chuck."

"And we still need to know what you know about Suzanne," Aunt Star stage-whispered at her.

"I said I'll be back." Callie walked a few booths down and began chatting with the two old men seated there. I recognized them as friends of my Grandpa

Charlie, who had passed away when I was a kid. The men were at least twice Callie's age, and I knew at least one man's wife was still alive, yet they flirted with her.

Very few men could resist Callie, with her dazzling green eyes, her long, blonde, feathered hair, and her even longer legs. It also didn't hurt that she left more blouse buttons undone than I would ever have the courage to.

Aunt Star waved a hand in front of my face. "Are you in there?"

I blinked and focused on her. "Sorry. I wonder what she knows about Suzanne."

"We'll soon find out. You'd better add her to the list of suspects. We don't know for sure she didn't do it."

As I wrote Suzanne's name, Aunt Star continued, "Tell me what you know about this Chuck guy."

"I don't want to have to tell it twice, so let's wait until Callie gets back."

She sighed. "Fine. I guess that makes sense." She paused. "Add him to your list. This isn't going to be as easy as I thought."

"You thought solving a murder would be easy?" I asked and added Chuck's name to my list.

"Maybe not easy, but perhaps not this complicated. I mean, who would have thought there could be this many suspects?"

"Anybody who has read or watched any mysteries."

"Excuse me for not being as well-read or watched as you," she retorted. I could tell she regretted her tone, but she didn't admit it, and I didn't call her out this time. Neither did I apologize for my sarcasm. I picked up a sweetener packet and squished it between my fingers.

Callie rang several customers up at the cash register. The late morning lull had hit, and only a few other people remained in their seats. Callie wiped down a recently vacated table, tossed the rag into a gray plastic tub behind the counter, and then slid in next to me. I moved over to give her room.

"I should have a few minutes now before the lunch crowd starts coming in. Spill."

"All I know is Chuck is one of the three guys that found me ... you know."

"When you found Aidan?" Callie diplomatically offered.

"Yes. It was him, Marty James, and Aidan's cousin Zane."

"Did he seem surprised?" Aunt Star asked.

"Hmm. Let me think."

I kept fiddling with the packet as I closed my eyes and thought back to the moment the men entered the kitchen. Before I could come to any conclusions about Chuck's state of mind, the packet burst open and sweetener flew everywhere. Callie swept up the mess into a pile with her hands while Aunt Star shook her head at me.

"Well …," Callie prompted.

"When I came to, I opened my eyes, and the first thing I saw was Marty. He and Zane helped me up. The other guy—Chuck—checked for a pulse. I remember wondering why, because it was obvious Aidan was dead."

"Maybe he was putting on a show," Callie said.

"Could be. When I recovered a bit from the shock, I told everyone to make sure and not touch anything. As we left the kitchen, I told Chuck to turn off the faucet, and I said to use a towel so he wouldn't leave any fingerprints.

"But I didn't watch him, and I may have given him the perfect opportunity either to wipe his prints or to leave prints he could explain away." I dropped my head into my hands. "I'm an idiot."

"No, you're not, honey," Callie said and wrapped an arm around me. She gently rubbed my arm. "You had no idea he might be a suspect."

I lifted my head when I remembered another detail. "Chuck is the one who told Shane what happened!"

"Seriously?" Callie asked.

"Yes, he went with me to the office to call 911, and we ran into Shane after that, and Chuck stopped to tell him while I headed back to the kitchen."

"That's a little crazy, if Chuck is the actual murderer," Aunt Star said. "What I don't understand is why he wasn't arrested, if he had a decent motive and the means and opportunity, but Suzanne *was* arrested. What do the cops have on her? It's your turn to spill, Callie Collister."

Callie settled back into her seat. "It seems Aidan had yet another woman in his life." She glanced at Aunt Star, who shook her head in exasperation. "Jacqui Storm."

"Are you kidding me?" Aunt Star said. "She's only been back in town for what? A month?"

"More like three," Callie said. The woman remembered everything.

"What's the deal, then?" I asked. "Why did Suzanne have a problem with that? And why was it a big enough problem to make her want to kill Aidan?"

"You know how Suzanne thinks laziness is the road that leads directly to hell?"

I nodded. If I wasn't actively typing or on the phone when Suzanne entered the church office, I got a lecture on that very topic.

"Within days of Jacqui moving back, Suzanne started harping at her to find a job. A couple weeks later, she got a job as the receptionist at Shane Patrick's new office."

"Really?" I asked as I grabbed another sweetener packet. Aunt Starla swatted it out of my hand and put it back in the holder.

I continued, "How did I not hear about that?"

"She didn't even last a day!" Callie said triumphantly.

"Ooooh," Aunt Starla said. "Why?"

"Shane caught her and Aidan together in the supply closet."

Aunt Starla groaned. "Can they be any more cliché?"

I cocked my head to the side. "Why would that make Suzanne mad enough to kill Aidan?"

Before Callie could respond, the diner bell jingled. Aunt Star looked over our heads and held up a finger to keep Callie from speaking. "It's Shane," she whispered.

TEN

I SWIVELED MY HEAD and watched Shane cross the cafe to the counter. I thought he was going to take a seat at one of the stools, but he stood by the cash register.

"He's picking up some food. I'll be right back." Callie stood.

"Find out what he knows," I whispered as she walked away.

She gave me a thumbs up.

Aunt Star said, "I would have thought the Patrick house would be overloaded with food by this point. Everybody would have taken them a dish."

"Yeah, that seems pretty strange."

"I hope Callie asks him some questions. We need more information."

"Aunt Star! The man is grieving his brother's death."

"Hey, I'm grieving too. And I'm guessing he wants the killer caught even more than we do."

"Shh," I shushed her. "I want to hear what they're saying."

"Callie's going to tell us everything when he's gone."

Light tapping on the window by our booth caused us both to turn our heads. Veronica was out on the sidewalk giving us a questioning look. I surreptitiously pointed across the restaurant to where Callie was chatting with Shane. Veronica spotted them and scurried toward the diner's door. I flipped my notebook shut and dropped it into my purse. The bell jingled, and Veronica soon slid in next to me.

"What's this?" Veronica motioned toward the pile of sweetener on the table. "It should have been cleaned up. You can't get good help these days."

"Callie was cleaning it up," Aunt Star said with clenched teeth, "when Shane came in. Did you want her to ignore him?"

Veronica huffed. "I guess not. We need more information. I got nowhere with the people at the hardware store and the dime store. People just come and go at the washateria, and the people doing their laundry in there today weren't there Saturday. The bank is closed on Saturday afternoons. I guess it's good they didn't see Suzanne." She pointed her thumb out the window. "Nobody was paying any attention to the street or the church until the cops showed up."

"Did you stop by McCoy's?" I asked.

McCoy's 66 gas station was situated at the corner of the four-way stop, catty-corner from the church. The station was owned by Trixie's dad, Marvin McCoy, and provided full service. Either Marvin, his brother Jerry, or one of the high school kids who worked there after school and on weekends would have been outside nearly all Saturday afternoon pumping gas, washing windshields, and checking oil levels.

"I did, but they said Cory Hankins started working there a couple weeks ago and was working the pumps on Saturday. He's at school, so we can't talk to him yet."

I sat up straight at the mention of Cory, and Aunt Star kicked me under the table. Veronica wasn't facing me, so she hadn't seen the change in my body language.

"What have you found out?" Veronica asked.

We didn't need tell her everything we knew. The last thing we needed was Veronica trying to control our entire investigation. I could tell Aunt Star was thinking the same thing and trying to figure out how much to tell her.

"To be honest ..." I instantly regretted my words, because the phrase usually precedes a half truth or even outright lie. I hoped Veronica didn't know that little bit of criminal psychology.

I started again, "We don't know a whole lot yet. Callie can't sit and chat very long. She has lots of tables to take care of."

Veronica made a show of looking at the entire diner, which was nearly empty.

"There were more people here a few minutes ago," I explained.

She sniffed in response.

I lowered my voice. "We've learned it's all to do with Jacqui."

"Jacqui? What's she got to do with it?"

I told Veronica what Callie had told us before Shane's entrance interrupted us. "We're waiting for her to come back and finish the story. And hopefully add to it with whatever she's coaxing out of Shane."

Callie knew when to flirt and when not to. This was a "not to flirt" situation. Yet she had other ways of getting people to talk. She was good at asking questions and paying attention to people's answers. My job has taught me that people will tell you almost anything when they know you'll listen.

Their conversation wrapped up, and Callie rang up Shane's order, grabbed a white paper bag from the pass-through window into the kitchen, and handed it to him. Shane spotted us as he was leaving and nodded. We all waved.

Callie returned to the booth. "I'm not going to have much time, so I'm going to talk, and you're going to listen, and then I gotta get ready for the lunch crowd."

"Understood," Aunt Star said. "We've filled Veronica in on what you told us about Suzanne and Jacqui."

"Great. Suzanne was upset with Jacqui for losing the job, and she was also mad at Aidan for being part of the problem. The following week, Suzanne got Jacqui an interview to be the part-time bookkeeper at the hardware store, but she missed the interview. Why? Aidan, again."

Veronica started to speak, but Callie held up a hand, and miraculously, Veronica hushed.

"Shane said Suzanne called Aidan multiple times and told him to stay away from Jacqui. Suzanne even made some threats, which likely made Aidan want Jacqui even more. Sorry, Star."

I did feel bad for Aunt Star. Sure, she was dating multiple people too, but Aidan took the cake. And Aunt Star must have still had some feelings for him, or she wouldn't have gone out with him.

"That's all I know," Callie said. "See you gals later." She stood, swept the pile of sweetener into her hand, and headed to the kitchen.

Veronica slumped in her seat and her face went

slack. This was a day for unexpected emotions from her.

"Maybe she did do it," she said.

"Veronica," I said, and she gave me a sharp look. "Mrs. Coker, you can't give up on Suzanne. It doesn't sound good for her, but do you truly think she could have done this?"

She sat up a little straighter. "No, I don't. That's going to be hard to prove, but we can do it." She paused. "Can't we?"

"Definitely."

———

WHEN I OPENED the office door upon our return, Greg and Pastor Coker shouted, "Happy birthday!" in unison. Greg presented me a cupcake with chocolate icing and colored sprinkles.

"It's your birthday?" Veronica asked. "I'm sorry. I should have remembered."

"Don't worry about it," I responded. "We've had enough to keep our minds occupied this morning." I turned to Greg. "Thank you for the cupcake." Then I turned to Pastor Coker and said, "And for the birthday greetings."

He bowed and said, "You're most welcome, my lady."

I giggled. Then I slipped off my coat and peeled the wrapper off my cupcake. I hadn't eaten anything yet and was famished.

"Why did we not get any food at the diner?" I said to no one in particular.

Greg slapped his forehead. "And why didn't I get anything else at the bakery?"

Veronica glared at him. I wasn't sure if that was because he hadn't gotten food or because he had left his post to run down the street to the bakery.

"Other things on our minds," Aunt Star said as she pulled one of the chairs by my desk to the center of the room and sat.

Veronica seemed put out that Aunt Star hadn't let her have the chair. She shot a pointed look at her husband, who dragged the other chair over for her. He leaned against the doorway into his office.

"Your mom called," Greg said to me. "That's how we were reminded of your birthday. She said to call her back."

I nodded and swallowed a mouthful of cupcake.

"Okay, what did everybody find out?" I asked.

Veronica stiffened at my initiative, but what was she going to do—repeat the question?

Pastor Coker told us Aidan's body was going to be released in the afternoon, which I knew but hadn't shared. Aidan's parents were not doing well, he said, so he didn't have the heart to question them about what Shane might have told the police about Suzanne.

I licked icing off my fingers in preparation for sharing my information, but Veronica jumped in and told the men what we had learned from Callie. She didn't mention she hadn't found out anything from the people in the shops.

We all turned to Greg, who was sitting on his desk. He took in a deep breath. "I learned something that's not good for Suzanne."

"Then spit it out," Veronica said.

"Minnie Jensen called," Greg said.

Veronica groaned, and with good reason. Minnie was a busybody, which was common in Cherry Hill. She was also an avowed atheist, which was not so common. She would argue theology with anyone who would take her on, which wasn't a whole lot of people. Suzanne could give her a run for her money, though. I smiled at the thought of the two of them going at it.

Greg continued, "She called to tell us something she thought we should know."

"Of course she did," Aunt Star said with a roll of her eyes.

I kept silent and picked crumbs from the cupcake liner. Pastor Coker disappeared into his office and soon returned pushing his rolling office chair. Aunt Star scooted her seat over to make room for him, and he plopped down. His chair rolled backward, but Veronica grabbed it and pulled it back into place.

When everyone was settled again, Greg said, "Minnie saw Suzanne Saturday afternoon."

"Great! She's got an alibi!" I said.

"Not so fast," he said. "Minnie saw her at the washateria."

Main Street Washateria, the local laundromat, sits next to The Check, directly across the street from the church office. I turned to look at it through the window by my desk.

Veronica had stopped in at the washateria this morning, but nobody works there. The owners unlock the door at 6:00 a.m. and lock it back up at 11:00 p.m. I didn't understand why Suzanne would be there, though. She could afford her own washer and dryer.

Veronica was thinking along the same lines. "Why was Suzanne there?" she asked. "She can do her laundry at home."

"Minnie said Suzanne's washing machine stopped working in the middle of a load, and Jacqui doesn't have a washer and dryer. She uses her mom's. And most of Suzanne's friends were at the wedding, so Suzanne had to go to the washateria."

I could imagine how embarrassed Suzanne would have been by the prospect of going to a laundromat. She would consider herself above doing her laundry in public.

"Wait a minute," I said. "Why wasn't Suzanne invited to the wedding?" She was in the same Sunday school class as Aidan's parents, so it was strange she wasn't invited.

"She was invited," Veronica said, "but she came up with a pitiful excuse not to go. I couldn't get her to tell me her actual reason. Now that I know about the situation between Jacqui and Aidan, I can imagine why."

Veronica turned back to Greg. "What else did Minnie say?"

"Minnie left the washateria while the wedding was letting out. Suzanne was still there, and she was alone."

We all pondered this new information for a few moments. Pastor Coker's chair creaked as he rocked back and forth.

"That doesn't sound good for Suzanne," Aunt Star said.

"Suzanne *did not* do this, and you know it, Starla Beckett," Veronica said with vehemence. I was half afraid she was going to smack Aunt Star.

"That's not what I said," my aunt retorted. "I said it doesn't sound good."

"She's right," I chimed in. "We now know Suzanne didn't have an alibi, and even worse, she had the perfect opportunity."

"The police might not know that," Pastor Coker said.

"Minnie said she told the police what she knew," Greg said.

I considered that information. "I wonder if she told them before or after Suzanne was arrested."

"Either way," Aunt Star said, "along with her motive, it makes her a prime suspect."

I knew Suzanne also had the means, though I still wasn't ready to share about the potential murder weapon with this entire group. Things didn't look good for our choir director. Plenty of other people also had motive, means, and opportunity, though. So why were the police so focused on Suzanne instead of one of them?

ELEVEN

AUNT STAR BOUGHT my birthday lunch from Dairy Queen, but we got it to-go so we could eat at home and discuss the case without anyone overhearing. As she drove us back to the house, I pulled my Dilly Bar out of the bag.

In between bites of chocolate-covered ice cream, I restated everything we knew about the case, with Aunt Star jumping in on occasion. We couldn't come to any conclusions about why Suzanne was a more viable suspect than anyone else on our list.

"We may have to wait until tonight to find out anything else," she said.

"Tonight? How will tonight help us?"

"Birthday drinks ... with Darren?"

"Oh yeah. You think he'll tell us anything?" I asked as I picked a chunk of chocolate from my shirt and popped it into my mouth.

"Probably not, but we can try."

Darren didn't drink, so we couldn't try to get him drunk and hope he'd spill the beans. Aunt Star had her ways of getting men to open up, but I wasn't sure I wanted to see them.

After lunch Aunt Star dropped me back off at the church. The afternoon dragged on, with lots of calls from curious church members but no more relevant information.

On Monday afternoons I typically checked all the Sunday school classrooms to make sure everything was in its place and to see if any supplies were running low. I couldn't do that and answer the phone, though, and nobody else was around.

The Cokers had gone home to the parsonage across the parking lot. The church phone line also rang over there, so they'd know if I didn't answer it. Pastor Coker wouldn't mind and would even answer it himself if it kept ringing, but his wife wouldn't answer on principle, since it was my job during office hours. Greg had left to grab a late lunch and then stop by a few places around town to see if he could learn anything new.

I sat and stared at the washateria through the window. I wondered if anyone else had gone in after Minnie left. Surely someone else had seen Suzanne there and could verify her whereabouts.

I couldn't stand not knowing what was happening any longer and called the Cokers' personal phone line at the parsonage. Veronica picked up.

Without any preamble I said, "Have you found out anything else?"

"Hello to you, too, Beckett."

I felt bad for being rude, but she had been rude right back, so I didn't respond.

"No, I haven't heard anything," she finally said. "I've tried calling Suzanne's number and going by her house to see if the police have let her go or if she's out on bail or something, but I got no response."

Since no one close to me had ever been arrested, I wasn't sure how long the police could keep people before charging them with a crime or letting them go. I doubted I could trust what I had learned from novels and TV shows. The police in those situations didn't usually follow the rules. Though I had no idea what the actual law was, if Suzanne was still at the police station, that wasn't good news for her.

"Did you try Jacqui?" I asked Veronica.

"She's not home, either, but school will be out soon, and her son will be coming home. I would hope she'd be home by then. Either that or she'll pick him up at school."

"Her car's not working," I reminded her.

"Ah, yes."

Neither of us spoke for a moment.

"Let me know if you hear anything," I said, and we hung up.

I drummed my fingers on my desk while considering my next move once Greg returned and I could leave the office. I did need to check the classrooms, but I'd rather be out talking to people and seeing if I could find any more clues. I pulled my notebook out of my purse and perused my suspect list again, hoping for inspiration.

The furnace kicked on, and air whooshed down from the vent above my head. I needed to ask Arnie to adjust the angle on it. The air lifted the notebook page for a moment, and I saw I had written something on the next page. I flipped to it and read aloud, "How did he die?"

I now knew part of that answer, but I didn't know exactly what the murder weapon was or where it was. I knew it probably wasn't in the kitchen, and it wasn't in the box of sports equipment.

I propped my chin on my hands and considered where the killer could have put the weapon. If the person had come from outside the church, they may have taken it with them. If it had been someone in the wedding party, they would have had to hide it somewhere in the building.

Greg entered the office before I could formulate my

search plan. He stood by my desk and ran his hand down the back of his hair, as if he were considering what he was about to say.

He opened his mouth twice before saying, "You look nice today."

My face heated, which meant it was now clashing with my new neon purple shirt. I had bought the top and multicolored skirt as a birthday present to myself the previous weekend.

"Thanks." I smiled at him.

The door opened again and hit Greg in the back. He stumbled and grabbed my desk to steady himself. I automatically reached out and grabbed his arm. His gaze shot to mine.

Pastor Coker profusely apologized. Greg reluctantly looked away from me, straightened, and gave his body a little shake.

"No need to apologize. I should have moved away from the door."

"Glad you're not hurt," Pastor Coker said from the doorway. "Look who I found at the church door!"

He stepped inside and Shane Patrick followed him in. After a moment of stunned silence, Greg and I greeted Shane and offered our condolences.

Pastor Coker said, "To what do we owe the pleasure, Sha— I mean, Dr. Patrick?"

"Uh, I wanted to talk about the funeral a bit," Shane said.

"Yes, yes, step into my office."

They shut the door most of the way but left a small gap. Greg caught my eye and nodded toward the door. I put my finger to my mouth and cupped my hand behind my ear. He smirked at me and picked up the phone. I wildly waved my arms. He silently laughed and put the receiver back down.

The men's voices were a bit muffled, so I moved out from behind my desk, opened a drawer of the file cabinet next to Pastor Coker's office door, and flipped through the files, in case the door suddenly opened.

My snooping didn't garner much information. Shane wanted to speak at the funeral, so the men talked about a few Bible verses he could use.

When the conversation seemed to be winding down, I quietly closed the file drawer and returned to my chair. The door opened a second later. Out of the corner of my eye I caught Greg wiping his brow. I stifled a grin and purposefully didn't turn toward him.

Shane soon left, and Pastor Coker sat in one of the guest chairs. We briefly discussed how hard it must be for Shane yet how inspiring it was that he wanted to speak at his brother's funeral.

Since I was no longer alone in the office, I could

now leave to search the building for the murder weapon. And I had the perfect excuse for doing so.

"I'm going to go do my weekly check of the classrooms. Can one of you answer the phone?"

"Will do," Greg said.

I thanked Greg, opened the door, and stumbled over my own feet. I put my hands out in preparation for hitting the floor, but I hit a person instead. I felt a sense of déjà vu. This time, however, the person caught me.

"Beckett, are you okay?" Greg had circled his desk in record time.

"I got her," Shane said as he helped me stand up straight.

"Dr. Patrick, you're back. Do you need something else?" Greg asked.

I wondered how Shane had gotten in, since the police had suggested keeping the church doors locked even when we were there.

Shane replied, "Uh, I needed to use the restroom before heading out. You good, Becky?"

"Sure. More embarrassed than anything."

Shane looked me up and down, as if assessing my physical ability to continue standing. He must have concluded I was fine, because he said goodbye and hurried out the door.

I headed in the opposite direction and decided to provide myself with a little suspense by starting with the rooms closest to the sanctuary and making my way toward the kitchen at the opposite end of the building. In my estimation, the weapon was more likely to be hidden closer to the kitchen than farther away—if it were in the building at all.

I searched every cupboard and drawer. I dug through every toy bin and inspected every closet. I even checked the pockets of the choir robes. They were deep pockets. I knew this not because I could carry a tune in a bucket, but because Juanita Anderson was always digging around in her pockets to find a tissue during the sermon. I would swear it often took her a full minute of rummaging around before she pulled one out.

When I entered the youth classroom, I realized this was the room where Chuck had informed Shane about Aidan's death. A chill ran through me at the realization. It didn't help that this room was a little colder than the others had been.

Most everything seemed to be in place, but the metal supply cabinet door was slightly ajar. There was a trick to shutting it, and whoever had been in the cabinet last didn't know the trick. I opened the door to see if I needed to restock any supplies.

"Beckett?"

I jerked in surprise and banged my hand on a shelf.

"Oh, no! I'm sorry," Greg said as he rushed toward me.

"Not your fault." I nursed my hand and tried to smile through the pain.

He stopped a few feet short of me. "Can you move it?"

I rotated my hand to make sure it wasn't broken and then shook it more vigorously. "I think it'll hurt for a while." I looked up. "Did you need something?"

Greg stared at me blankly.

"Why did you come in here?" I asked.

"You'd been gone longer than you usually are when you check the classrooms. After you almost fell, I was concerned you had a delayed reaction or something." He laughed. "I realize how silly that sounds."

"No, it's fine. It's good to be cautious. While you're here, do you need any more supplies or anything?"

"Nope, got plenty of everything. If you're sure you're okay, I'll leave you to it."

I nodded and he started back toward the door but then spun back toward me—a move my bad leg would have never allowed me to make. "By the way," he pointed at the cabinet, "do you know why there's a baseball bat in there?"

TWELVE

MY BODY STIFFENED.

"What's wrong?" Greg asked.

"There was a baseball bat?"

"Yes."

"In the cabinet?"

"Yeeeees," he said, as if talking to someone who was a little slow to catch on.

"And it wasn't there before?"

"No. We don't keep sports equipment in here. You know that. I thought it was strange for you to put a bat in the cabinet last week when you made your rounds."

"I didn't put it there," I said.

He frowned. "So why did you act weird when I mentioned it?"

I sat at the nearest table and motioned for Greg to join me. I told him what Frank had said about the murder weapon and what I had found—or not found—on my search earlier in the day.

Greg's brow furrowed, and he put his hand on mine. "Beckett, are you trying to solve this murder?"

"Yes, why?" I slowly pulled my hand away. I didn't mind his gesture in principle, but I could tell by his tone he didn't think I should—or perhaps could—figure out who killed Aidan.

"Because it's dangerous, that's why!" He slapped his hand on the table in emphasis. "There's a murderer running around Cherry Hill. If they know you're trying to find them, you could be their next victim. What are you thinking?"

"I'm *thinking* Aidan's parents and brother need answers. And I'm thinking I'm going to help them get those answers. I also want to clear Suzanne's name." And Aunt Star's, but I didn't mention that to him.

"That's what the police are for!" He ran a hand through his hair in frustration.

"Have we not been spending this entire day trying to help clear Suzanne's name?" I asked.

"Yes, but that's not the same as finding the killer!"

I explained my reasoning that the best way to clear Suzanne was to find the real murderer.

Greg thought for a second and said, "I guess that makes sense, especially since things don't look too good for Suzanne."

"Exactly," I said with no small amount of sarcasm.

I needed to calm down. He was only looking out for me. I took a deep breath and apologized.

"Now, where did you put the bat?"

"What do you mean? I left it there. The kids were starting to arrive, so I left it where it was, and I thought you must have had a good reason for putting it there."

"It's not there now," I said.

Greg stepped to the cabinet and opened both doors wide. He dropped to his knees and swept his hand all the way to the back of the bottom shelf. He slowly turned to me. "You're right. It's gone."

I rolled my eyes. I already knew that. "Let's check the rest of the room to make sure one of the kids didn't put it somewhere else."

It didn't take long to search all the places big enough to conceal a bat.

"We should tell the police about this," Greg stated.

I'd already had this conversation with myself. "Yeah, but what do we tell them? We thought a bat was missing, but maybe it wasn't, but then again, maybe it is? They'll laugh. And they'll tell me yet again to not get involved."

"They might, but it could be a clue."

"I don't know." I paused. "How about this? Darren is supposed to be at The Blue Barn tonight for my birthday thing. If he's there—but I'm doubtful in the middle of this investigation—we can slip it into the conversation."

Greg surveyed me for several seconds before agreeing.

"I also think you should know there are people who think your aunt did this," Greg said.

"Ugh. Still? Even with Suzanne in jail—or wherever she is at the moment?"

"Yes. And I shouldn't say this, but Veronica is one of them."

I groaned. "I don't know why I'm surprised by that." I was, however, absolutely angered by it. I took several deep breaths to calm down. "She's trying to deflect blame from Suzanne. At least that's what I'm going to choose to believe."

———

AFTER WORK, I drove straight to my parents' house. Aunt Star was meeting us there after a house showing.

I pulled into the drive behind my dad's old black Ford pickup and steeled myself before I got out of the car. I was never sure what my mother's mood would be, especially if Aunt Star was present. Mom could be judgmental when she chose to be, which was more often than I'd like. Though when would I like it? But she could also be completely personable.

I stepped out of the car and traversed the cracked

sidewalk leading to the front door of the small, white, wood-paneled house my parents had bought when they got married. As I climbed the three steps to the small concrete front porch, the door swung open. Dad had been watching for me.

He hugged me and wished me a happy birthday. I moved into the kitchen, where Mom was hovering over a skillet at the stove. She turned and gave me a quick smile as I crossed to her and gave her a side hug.

"What can I do to help?"

"Nothing. You're the birthday girl, so relax."

Since I wasn't going to argue with that, I took a seat at the Formica-topped kitchen table.

Mom turned and pointed her spoon at me. "I have one rule for tonight."

I tried my hardest to not roll my eyes.

"No talk of murder, you hear me? Let's enjoy the evening."

That was fine with me. I needed a break from thinking about it. And since Mom had Mondays off from her part-time job as a teller at Cherry County Bank, she wouldn't have as much gossip to pass on as usual.

Dad joined me at the table. We spent a few minutes talking about his day. His job with the county road department was rarely filled with excitement, and this day was no exception.

Brrrrring!

Dad reached over and grabbed the phone off the wall. Shortly after his greeting, he handed the phone out to me. I looked at him questioningly.

"Your niece would like to speak with you."

I snatched the phone from him. "Jodie! How are you, kiddo?"

My six-year-old niece lived in Chicago with her two-year-old brother Brandon, my brother Rafe, and his wife Cari. Rafe attended the University of Illinois on a baseball scholarship and immediately after graduation got a job as a financial analyst at a firm in downtown Chicago.

Jodie sang the birthday song to me and chattered about her day at school. She then coached Brandon to say, "Happy birthday," to me, which sounded more like a totally adorable "Abby birdie." I then spoke to Cari briefly before Rafe wrapped up the call. By the time I got off the phone, Aunt Star had arrived.

Dinner was tacos and rice, with a side of apples. My mother cannot fix a meal without fruit. She had also baked me a chocolate cake covered with white, fluffy icing. It was topped not with twenty-eight individual candles, thankfully, but with large candles in the shape of a 2 and 8.

The candles were easy to blow out, after I silently made my wish of solving Aidan's murder. The wish would have been silent even without the dinnertime ban on talking about the murder or the tradition that if you say your birthday wish out loud, it won't come true. Dad would have a stroke if he thought his little girl might be doing something potentially unsafe.

When we finished eating our cake, Mom handed me a gift. I knew it would be a shirt from Hang It Up, the clothing store downtown. It always was. And it was never a shirt I would wear.

I tore off the wrapping paper and opened the box to reveal a light pink, short-sleeved, button-up shirt with white vertical pinstripes. The shirt itself was fine, and at least the stripes weren't horizontal, which is never flattering. However, the woman who had given birth to me should know light pink is not my color. No pink is my color. I stifled a sigh and thanked my parents for the gift. I'd make sure to wear it to their house at least once.

Aunt Star pretended to have forgotten to bring my gift, but I knew she was faking it. It was bound to be something nice, and she didn't want to show up my parents.

My aunt and I soon took our leave, so we could get home and change out of our work clothes before meeting the others at The Blue Barn. When we arrived home, Aunt Star handed me a card and gift-wrapped box. The card detailed a one-hundred-dollar shopping spree with her at Capital Mall in Jefferson City. The gift was a pair of bright green jelly shoes she knew I'd had my eye on.

I was grateful both for the gifts and for Aunt Star not giving them to me in my parents' presence. I gave her a giant hug, and we each disappeared into our rooms to get ready for the evening.

A night out on the town in Cherry Hill was never a fancy event. Nobody at the bar would be wearing dressy clothes. In fact, most of them would be wearing whatever they wore to work that day, even if it was mechanic's coveralls. However, it was my birthday, and I was going to look nice.

I stared at the clothes in my closet for a minute and then started pulling items out, holding them up to me in front of the full-length mirror on the closet door and tossing them into two piles on my bed: a no pile and a maybe pile.

Finally, I settled on a pair of acid-washed Lee jeans and an oversized red, blue, and yellow color-blocked United Colors of Benetton shirt Aunt Star had given me for Christmas. I added layered red and yellow socks and slipped into some bright blue Keds.

I tried tight rolling my jeans, which I'd seen in a magazine, but upon inspection in the mirror, I decided I looked silly. I unrolled them and tucked the hems into my socks instead.

Aunt Star appeared in my bathroom doorway as I was finishing my makeup. She looked fabulous, as usual, in a pair of navy slacks and a white, silky button-up blouse. Aunt Star didn't do casual. Yet somehow, she never seemed out of place when she was dressed much nicer than anyone else in the room.

While I added the finishing touches to my light blue eye shadow, I filled her in on everything I'd learned since lunch. Then I hooked in some dangly bright blue earrings, unearthed my purse from under the pile of clothes on my bed, and was ready to go.

Three minutes later we pulled into a parking spot on Main Street next to Trixie's brown Ford Bronco. Despite her name, Trixie was not a "girly-girl." A few families in town had bought one of those new ridiculous-looking minivans, but not Trixie. She would be hauling her kids around in the Bronco until the day it died.

The Blue Barn, contrary to its name, was not blue, nor did it even closely resemble a barn. The bar was housed in an old brick two-story building much the same as the others in downtown Cherry Hill.

The sounds of Bon Jovi's "Runaway" filtered out before we even opened the door. When we entered, the smell of cigarette smoke almost overwhelmed me. The place was packed for a Monday night. I quickly spotted Greg, who waved us over to a large, round table on a small stage in the back corner.

On weekend nights, the stage held a live band or deejay, but during the week, the owners filled the space with a few tables. Though I didn't like feeling on display being higher than the rest of the crowd, it usually was quieter there, so I couldn't complain.

We wove through the tables, saying hi to people as we made our way to our friends. Darren was the only one of the group who had yet to arrive. Trixie gave me an awkward hug, and we both wished each other a happy birthday. When we were kids, I rarely let her forget I was older than her by exactly one day. Now I claimed we were the same age.

Greg stood awkwardly for a moment as if considering whether he would hug me or not. In the end, he pulled out the chair between his and Trixie's for me. Aunt Star wiggled her eyebrows while I ignored her.

The waitress stepped onto the stage. "Happy birthday, Becky."

I peered at her through the smoky haze. "Hi, Marcie.

Thanks." Marcie was a few years behind me in school. I hadn't seen her in the bar before.

"What'll everybody have?" she asked.

I wasn't much of a drinker, but it was my birthday, so I ordered a Bud Light. The others placed their orders, and Aunt Star ordered an RC Cola for Darren.

My back was to the door, so when the noise in the bar suddenly got quieter, I turned around to see why. Darren and another man were heading our way. When people realized Darren was there for personal reasons instead of police business, they returned to their conversations. It must be strange to have that kind of power over entire rooms.

I couldn't see the other guy's face until the two men reached us and Darren moved to the side to grab an extra chair from the table next to us. The man didn't look familiar, but from the way he carried himself, I decided he was a policeman, had been in the military, or both.

His dark hair was cut short but not quite a buzz cut, and his cheekbones could have cut glass. Even through his long-sleeved shirt you could tell he was fit. He wasn't classically good-looking like Aidan or Darren, and he wasn't as tall, but a pleasurable ripple shot through me when our eyes met. He held my gaze for a few moments until Darren spoke.

"I hope the birthday girl doesn't mind, but I invited Mitchell to join us. He's a detective on loan from Jeff City during the murder investigation."

"I don't mind at all," I said, in a much sultrier voice than I had intended. Aunt Star let out a choking cough, and Mitchell gave me a smile that could melt butter. Greg's fingertips brushed my upper back as he rested his hand on the back of my chair.

Darren slid the extra chair in, and everyone shifted to make more room for Mitchell while making introductions.

"Since Mitchell doesn't know anyone in town," Darren said, "I thought I'd give him the option of coming here with us instead of watching TV in his room at The Osh."

The Oak Street Hotel, otherwise known as "The Osh," was a quaint little hotel around the corner. The Napier family had owned and operated the business for over a hundred years.

Mitchell held his hands out like he was weighing two options. "It was a tough choice: either this or *Scarecrow and Mrs. King,"* he said with a laugh.

"I'm no Kate Jackson," I said with a dazzling smile, "but I hope I'm more fun."

"I'm sure you are," he said with a wink.

Greg cleared his throat and said, "How are things

going with the investigation?"

"Yes," I added, "what's happening with Suzanne?"

The two policemen looked at each other for a few seconds, and I leaned forward in anticipation. Mitchell gave Darren a slight nod.

Darren turned back to the rest of us and said, "It'll be on the 10:00 news tonight, so I might as well tell you. Suzanne has officially been charged with Aidan's murder."

Mine was not the only gasp at the table. I figured they would have been able to clear her or would at least have rounded up another suspect or two to investigate before charging her.

"What about the murder weapon?" Greg asked. "You don't have that, do you?"

Darren shot him an odd look. "Yes, we do."

THIRTEEN

I SAT BACK IN my chair and let out a long breath. "You found the bat?"

Darren narrowed his eyes at me. "What are you talking about?"

I had to think fast. He did not need to know the bat saga. "Uh, well, I figured, since Suzanne is so short and Aidan was so tall, the murder weapon had to have been a long object, if he was hit on the head."

"How do you know he was hit on the head?" Darren inquired.

I cocked my head at him.

"Oh. Yes. You were there."

"What?" Mitchell looked from Darren to me and back again.

I was surprised Darren hadn't told Mitchell who I was when he'd invited him. I'd give Mitchell a few more seconds to figure it out. Everyone else seemed to have the same idea, because no one said a word.

"Ahhh, Beckett. Also known as Becky Monahan. You're the one who found Mr. Patrick," he said.

"Yes," I said with a sigh and an eye roll. "It seems like a losing game to get people in this town to stop calling me Becky."

Aunt Star said, "This is all very fascinating, but let's get back to the murder weapon."

Darren shifted in the straight-backed wooden chair to get more comfortable before tipping it onto its back legs and saying, "When we searched Suzanne's house this morning, we found a rolling pin under some clothes in a laundry basket. The medical examiner's report stated the murder weapon was a cylindrical object made of wood. It's pretty clear cut."

The rest of us sat in stunned silence for a few moments.

I asked, "Were her fingerprints on the rolling pin?"

"It had been wiped clean," Mitchell answered. "I doubt I have to tell you that's pretty suspicious. No blood, either."

Why would Suzanne wipe the rolling pin clean yet keep it in her house? The facts weren't adding up, but I wasn't about to question the police—especially when Darren had told me multiple times to keep out of the investigation.

Marcie stopped by the table to check on us, and we ordered baskets of fries to go with our drinks. The conversation then turned to more lighthearted topics.

At one point, while the rest of us were debating the Beach Boys' original version of "California Girls" versus David Lee Roth's cover, which was playing on the jukebox, I noticed Aunt Star having a quiet tete-a-tete with Darren. Her eyes brimmed with tears, and he had moved his chair closer and draped his arm around her. His long fingers lightly stroked her shoulder.

I could imagine they were talking about Aidan. With all my focus on finding his killer, I had nearly forgotten how much he had meant to my aunt. I could kick myself for that. And I was impressed by Darren comforting her instead of continuing to be angry with her about dating another man.

Trixie, meanwhile, peppered Mitchell with questions. We learned he grew up in a small town about an hour away, and he had played a couple of high school football games against Cherry Hill High. After graduation, he joined the Marines, and when he returned, he joined his local police force before taking a job as a detective in Jefferson City a few years later. Due to his experience with major crimes as well as his knowledge of small towns, he was often sent to help smaller police departments with high-profile cases.

I wondered if his experience included people being framed, because that was clearly happening here. I legitimately couldn't believe Suzanne was guilty, and the rolling pin thing didn't make sense. As we walked out of the bar, I found my chance to mention it.

"Mitchell," I said, "have you ever been involved in a case where someone was framed for a crime they didn't commit?"

We approached Aunt Star's car and he opened my door. "I once investigated a bank robbery where all signs pointed toward the suspect being framed."

I nodded as I slipped into my seat.

He continued, "In the end, we discovered he was framing himself to try to put us off the scent."

Mitchell hadn't needed to think before answering, which meant this wasn't a memory pulled from the recesses of his mind. He had been thinking about it, and he believed that's what Suzanne had done.

He was wrong.

I almost said as much, but he leaned down so his face was even with mine, rested his hand on my shoulder, and spoke again. "It was great to meet you, *Beckett.* I'm sure I'll see you again." He smiled and closed the door.

My shoulder tingled all the way home.

Aunt Star pulled into the garage and turned off the engine, but instead of waiting to close the overhead door with the button on the garage wall, she hit the remote in the car. I turned to her with a questioning look.

She pulled the key out of the ignition and pointed it over her shoulder. "I think someone might have been following us. I could see the same vehicle about a block behind us all the way here."

My eyes widened. "Are you going to call Darren?"

"I don't think so. I'm sure I'm overreacting. Lots of people live in this part of town, including several people at the bar who might have left the same time we did."

She made a good point. If she didn't think it was worth calling Darren, I wasn't going to push it. Still, I felt a bit uneasy about the situation. When we got inside the house, I made sure all the doors were locked, including the one leading into the garage, which I could never recall locking. I didn't even have a key for it.

After I crawled into bed, I lay on my back listening to the sounds of the night. Nothing seemed amiss, so I rolled over onto my side and went to sleep.

———

THE NEXT MORNING, I called Trixie first thing to wish her a happy birthday. The kids had brought her toast and orange juice in bed, and Scott was getting the two of them ready for school as part of his gift to her.

Eight-year-old Krystal was self-sufficient for her age, but six-year-old Victor was another matter. He and Scott were arguing about shoes in the background.

I stretched the phone cord across the room so I could reach the coffee maker and start a pot brewing.

"So," Trixie said, "Mitchell." She was a woman of few words.

"What about Mitchell?"

I wrapped my robe more tightly around me and sat at the table. It was a little chilly in the kitchen. For the hundredth time, I wished for a phone in my bedroom. Aunt Star claimed the process of adding a phone jack in my room was more trouble and cost than it was worth. I disagreed, but it wasn't my house.

Trixie said, "He and Greg were eyeing each other warily all evening."

"Warily? Who uses that word in real life?"

"I do. And you might have a love triangle situation going on."

I laughed. "I don't think so."

"Greg kept looking at you when 'Can't Fight This Feeling' was playing on the jukebox. And he was *not* happy you were chatting with Mitchell as we left the bar. I think he was hoping to offer to drive you home, but you didn't give him a chance."

"I didn't know he wanted a chance."

"Do you like him?" she asked bluntly.

"Sure, I like him. He's a nice guy."

"That's not what I mean."

I sighed. "I know. I do like him. He's kind, cute, and he thinks he's funny even though he's not, which I oddly find endearing. I don't think I want to date him, though. Since we work together, it would be weird if we did, don't you think?"

The coffee was ready, so I got up to pour a cup.

"Maybe. But what I like about him for you is he doesn't seem to be broken."

My obsession with helping people can sometimes be good, but that trait has historically been detrimental when it comes to men. I'm often attracted to men who need help—who I think need "fixing," as Trixie had alluded to. I had even found myself engaged to one of those men. Thankfully I had come to my senses before walking down the aisle with him.

"I think you're right." I poured cream and sugar into my mug. "He seems to be a normal guy."

She was silent for a moment. "Is normal what you want? You don't need broken, but would you find normal to be boring?" My friend knew me well.

I leaned against the counter and blew on my coffee.

"Probably, but you don't find many not-normal guys in Cherry Hill. All the interesting ones leave and don't come back. Maybe I should give Greg a chance."

"What about Mitchell?"

I sighed again, but this one was accompanied by a smile. "He might not be boring. I would definitely say yes to a date with him." I paused. "He doesn't live here, though."

"You know I'd miss you if you left Cherry Hill again, but Jeff City isn't that far away."

"I'm not moving anywhere. I met him last night!"

"You're the one who brought up where he lives. I'm trying to be logical."

"Which is to be expected."

Trixie was nothing if not logical. It's what made her a great math teacher.

The line crackled, and Trixie's voice sounded muffled. "Scott's losing control of the kids, so I better go. Thanks for the birthday call."

We hung up as Aunt Star swept in, dressed in blue jeans, a fuzzy pink sweater, and a pair of brown leather loafers. The outfit was much more low-key than her usual work wear.

"What's with the jeans?"

Before answering, she poured herself a cup of coffee and took a gulp. No sweeteners or blowing for her.

"I'm going casual because I'm helping a client figure out what to do with her yard before we put the house on the market next month. We may need to get our hands dirty."

I would have worn my rattiest jeans, sweatshirt, and tennis shoes for that task.

"Why aren't you getting ready?" she asked.

"Headed that way now." I rinsed my coffee cup and placed it in the sink. "Had to call Trixie first and wish her a happy birthday."

VERONICA WAS WAITING for me at church.

"You're late."

"By one minute. Did I miss anything exciting?"

She huffed. "Did you know Suzanne was charged with murder?"

"I heard."

She frowned slightly. "Did you know the funeral is tomorrow, and the Patrick family decided not to hold it here because Suzanne is our choir director?"

I tilted my head. "No." That decision didn't make sense, but the Patricks wouldn't be thinking clearly.

Veronica didn't try to hide her smile of satisfaction that she knew something I didn't. I brushed past her, made a show of taking off my jacket and hanging it on the coat rack, and took my seat.

"Is there something I can help you with, Mrs. Coker?"

She put her hands on her hips. "This is a slight to First Community. It is not our fault Aidan got himself killed on our premises or the police are incompetent enough to think Suzanne did it. The nerve of those men!" She balled her hands into fists.

I didn't disagree with her, but I hated to let her know that. "She had the means, motive, and opportunity. The police think the evidence is very clear."

"It's as clear as cake, if you ask me," she said. "Why on earth would someone clean and then keep the murder weapon *in their own home?* It's crazy. Someone is trying to frame Suzanne. You can take that to the bank."

The bank. Amidst all the excitement, I had forgotten to take the Sunday offering deposit to the bank yesterday. I hoped the stack of bills and cash still sat inside the small safe bolted to the floor in the inner office. I'd take it as soon as Veronica left. No need for her to know I'd failed to do that simple yet essential task.

Veronica waved her hand in front of my face. "Earth to Beckett."

I shook my head to clear it. "Sorry. I think you're right."

She peered down at me. "You do?"

"I was thinking the exact same thing last night. Someone is trying to pin this on Suzanne."

She pulled a chair up to my desk and perched on the edge of it. "But who?"

How much should I tell her? I wavered for a moment but then decided she needed to know everything now that Suzanne was officially behind bars. We had to get her out. I wasn't afraid for her. I was more afraid for the wardens and other inmates. I had no doubt the woman would have the entire place under her thumb by the end of the day.

I cleared a space on my desk between Veronica and me, pulled my notebook out of my purse, and set it down facing her.

"What's this?" she asked as she opened it. When her brain registered the word "suspects" at the top of the first page, her eyes widened. When she saw Suzanne's name on the list, her face turned red. I grabbed a pen and scribbled out the name.

"Sorry," I said. "I had to add her until I knew for sure."

Veronica took in a few deep breaths but quickly calmed down.

I then told her everything I knew, from start to finish: what happened at the wedding, what I had learned from the police, the missing baseball bat, and all the suspects she didn't know about.

When I finished, she grabbed another pen and uncapped it. I slapped my hand down on the notebook to block her from writing.

"You had better not be adding my aunt's name to this list."

We stared at each other for a few seconds.

"No, I'm not," she said.

"Good."

"I will admit I had a moment of doubt about her, but I know she wouldn't have done it. I wasn't thinking straight yesterday. I was ready to blame anyone other than Suzanne."

I could understand that. I was ready to blame anyone but my aunt.

She held up the pen. I moved my hand and watched as she wrote a name in her flowing cursive handwriting: Jacqui Storm.

I chewed my pinky nail as I considered that addition. "Are you sure?"

"Why not?" Veronica said. "Maybe she got mad Aidan didn't invite her to the wedding, or she was angry with him about something else. She might have found out about all the other women in Aidan's life, which would be a decent motive."

"But would she frame her own mother for murder?" I couldn't imagine such a thing.

Veronica pressed her lips together for a moment. "There are things you do not know about Jacqui."

"Would you like to share?"

"No. We'll leave it at that."

I considered whether to push her on it but then remembered who I was talking to. "I'll take your word for it. Jacqui may have had motive, anyone could have had the means, but what about opportunity? How did she get here? Her car broke down."

"It stopped running Sunday morning," she said, jabbing her finger on my desk with each word. "Suzanne told me. It was Jacqui's excuse for not coming to church."

"It's hard to believe she would frame Suzanne."

"You can't expect a murderer to act like a normal person."

"True," I responded. "And she would have easy access to Suzanne's house to plant the rolling pin."

I drummed my fingers on the desk while we both thought.

"You know," I continued, "whoever did this— whether Jacqui or someone else—must be someone who knows Suzanne. A stranger wouldn't know enough to be able to frame her."

We grabbed for the pen simultaneously. Veronica won. She crossed Tonya, Nathan, and Chuck's names off the list with a flourish. "Now we're talking!" she said. "Narrowing down our suspects."

Only three names remained on the list: Jacqui Storm, Cory Hankins, and parking lot guy. The still-unknown man could very well have been Chuck or Nathan, but we didn't know for sure. I sighed as I put my finger by Cory's name. I hated to think Jacqui would frame her own mother, but I'd rather it be her than Cory.

"Surely it's not Cory," Veronica said.

"I hope not, too, but we can't cross him off yet." I held up a finger. "One: He would have known Aidan was at the wedding." I held up a second finger. "Two: He was working at the gas station across the street, so he would have had opportunity." I held up a third finger. "And three: He could have easily seen Suzanne down the street. Her new Caddy is very recognizable."

Veronica flipped my pinky up. "Four: He was very angry with Aidan." She pulled my thumb out. "And five: he's familiar enough with the church to have hidden the bat and then somehow gotten it out of the building during church yesterday morning. He was here. I saw him."

My heart sank. "And the bat was in the youth room—the room he knows the best."

I had all but convinced myself Cory was the killer when Veronica cut into my thoughts.

"How would he have been able to put the rolling pin into Suzanne's laundry basket?"

"Yes, that's the tricky part. And it's the part that makes Jacqui the prime suspect still." I chewed my pinky nail for a moment. "But how would Jacqui have gotten the bat out of the church, if her car wasn't working on Sunday? We know the bat was in the cabinet Sunday morning."

"All we know is Jacqui *says* her car broke down. She could be lying," Veronica said.

"Maybe the bat has nothing to do with it, and the rolling pin *is* the murder weapon," I said.

"Or she could have walked. It's quite a ways, and she would have had to leave Parker at home. I wouldn't put that past her. Disgraceful girl."

Disgraceful ... the word rang a bell. Where had I heard it recently? I scrunched my eyes shut to try to bring up the memory. I sucked in a big breath and smacked my hand down on the desk. Veronica jerked back.

"What?" she demanded.

"I had a conversation with Suzanne on Sunday morning. Right here." I smacked the desk again. "She told me my desk was a disgrace!"

"If the shoe fits ..." Veronica said.

"No, no, that doesn't have anything to do with anything. Suzanne was pumping me for information, asking what I knew, what the police knew. She was furious that I wouldn't tell her anything." I paused for effect. "What if she knew Jacqui did it?"

Veronica's eyes widened. "And now she's taking the fall for her daughter! They could have even planned it this way—Suzanne sacrificing herself."

"She is one of the most loyal people I know." To the people she likes, that is. She'd tell the rest of us to go fly a kite.

My leg started aching from sitting too long, so I got up and paced.

"That doesn't explain the bat, though," I said. "If the bat was the real murder weapon—and why all the disappearing if not—why wasn't it hidden in the laundry basket instead of the rolling pin, if this was all a big scheme cooked up by Jacqui and Suzanne?" I stopped pacing and leaned back against Greg's desk. "I don't think that's what happened. If it was Jacqui, Suzanne didn't know," I paused, "but she may suspect it."

"Why don't we ask Suzanne?" Veronica asked. Why not, indeed?

FOURTEEN

VERONICA INSISTED ON DRIVING us the two blocks to the police station. Then we raced each other to the door. She was in her usual take-charge mode, and she wasn't used to me challenging that. For once, I wasn't willing to step aside.

Barbara eyed us suspiciously when we approached her desk at a near run. "What?" she said, with no other greeting.

"We're here to see Suzanne," I blurted before Veronica could.

"You do realize she's been charged with murder," Barbara said flatly.

"Yes, and we want to talk to her," Veronica said. "We won't take—"

I nudged her none too lightly to stop her from finishing that sentence. Antagonizing Barbara wouldn't get us anywhere.

Barbara pursed her lips. "If you haven't noticed, this is not the jail."

We were idiots. The jail was attached to the

courthouse a few blocks away.

"I guess we'll head down there, then," I said.

"She's not there."

I refrained from rolling my eyes.

"Then where is she?" Veronica demanded.

"She's still in a holding cell here while they wait to get the jail paperwork processed. It's being held up because the four women's cells are full right now." She paused and smirked at us. "But I'm sure they'll soon find space for a murderer."

I grabbed Veronica's arm to keep her from launching herself across Barbara's desk.

"Can we see her?" I asked in an even tone of voice.

"Probably not, but I'll ask," Barbara said with a huff as she stood. "Stay here."

When she returned a minute later, she pointed her thumb into the pit and said, "Go see Frank."

Frank's desk was at the far end of the pit, outside Darren's office. I was glad most of the other desks were empty, as was Darren's office. We were much more likely to convince Frank to let us see Suzanne if Darren wasn't there to intervene. Frank set two metal folding chairs by his desk as we approached.

"Tell me why you ladies want to see Suzanne."

Veronica and I looked at each other. We hadn't talked about our official reason for visiting Suzanne.

We couldn't very well say we wanted to ask her if she was taking the fall for her daughter.

To fill the silence I said, "We want to check on her. See if she needs anything."

"And we want to pray with her," Veronica added.

That was the exact right thing to say. Frank had seemed skeptical of my reasons, but he was not about to deny a pastor's wife's request to pray with someone.

"Well, now, I think we can give you a couple minutes with her," Frank said as he stood. "Come with me."

We followed him through a thick, red metal door into a short hallway. Each side of the hall held a gray metal door with a tall, narrow window in it. Frank pulled out a set of keys and opened the door on the right.

"You get five minutes," he said and motioned us inside.

Suzanne was not looking any worse for wear after having been detained for more than twenty-four hours. She was wearing green polyester pants and a flowered shirt, which surprised me. I don't know what I expected, but it was disconcerting to see her in her normal clothes in such a place.

She rose from the bed and wrapped Veronica in her

arms. The door clanged shut behind us and I jumped slightly.

The holding cell was bigger than I had imagined. It held a metal bed frame that was bolted to the floor, topped with a thin mattress. A gray blanket lay folded at the end of the bed. The room included a toilet and sink but no mirror.

The two women pulled apart and Suzanne grabbed me into a hug as well. It was hard to breathe, but I hugged her back. I wasn't going to remind her she wasn't my biggest fan.

As there were no chairs in the cell, I let the two older women sit on the bed while I leaned against the wall near them. The cold soon seeped through my shirt from the cement blocks, so I adjusted my stance.

"We only have about four minutes left, so let's talk," I said.

"Suzanne," Veronica said as she took her friend's hand, "who do you think did this?"

Suzanne burst into tears. Between sobs she said, "I'm so glad you don't think I did it!"

"Of course we don't!" I said. "You were clearly framed. We need to talk about who might have done it, but we don't have much time."

She nodded and dabbed her face with the edge of the gray blanket. I tipped my head toward Veronica. I wasn't about to be the one to ask her.

Veronica took a deep breath and asked, "Did Jacqui do this?"

I focused on Suzanne's face so I could see her initial reaction to the question. She flinched and then her whole body drooped.

"Is that what people think?" she asked.

"Is that what *you* think?" I asked.

"I don't know. I hope not. A noise woke me in the middle of the night Sunday, but I didn't hear anything else, so I went back to sleep. That's when somebody must have gotten into the house to plant the rolling pin. I told the cops, but they said there was no indication of a break-in. So either I left a window unlocked, which I accidentally do sometimes, or the person had a key." She paused. "Jacqui has a key."

Tears streamed down Suzanne's face again.

I looked at my watch. "We have about a minute left. Why did the police question you in the first place?"

"They said they got a tip." She sighed. "I want to tell you to find who did this, but not if it's Jacqui! I don't want her to go to jail. If she does, Parker will have to go back to his dad in California, and I can't let that happen. He is not a good man."

Veronica said, "I understand that, but I won't let you get put away for a murder you didn't commit."

"That's right," I said. "And we don't know it *was* Jacqui. We're going to keep investigating, since the police won't be. They think they've solved this case, so they will have stopped looking for or questioning other suspects."

A key rattled in the lock and the door opened. "Time's up," Frank said.

"Oh!" Veronica said. "We haven't prayed yet."

"Make it quick," he said.

Veronica said a brief prayer for Suzanne, and we both hugged her before we stepped out. I jumped again when the door clanged shut.

Barbara glared at us as we walked through the lobby, but none of us spoke.

A police cruiser pulled up as we approached Veronica's sedan.

"Ladies," Darren said through his open window, "what are you doing here?"

I sent Veronica a panicked look over the top of the car. He wasn't going to be happy we'd talked to Suzanne.

Veronica stood tall, straightened her shoulders, and said, "We wanted to pray with Suzanne. Harold wasn't available," she cleared her throat, "so the two of us came to represent the clergy."

She was good, I'd give her that. I nodded in solidarity.

"That was kind of you," a masculine voice said.

I leaned down so I could see Mitchell in the passenger seat. Darren let out an exasperated breath, but Mitchell grinned at me.

"Nice to see you again, Beckett."

I gave him a winning smile. "You, too, Mitchell, er, Officer ... Detective?"

"Mitchell is fine," he said.

Darren sighed and rolled his eyes. "Are we done here?"

"Yes. See you gentlemen later."

"Have a good day, officers!" Veronica called out cheerily before she slid into the car and slammed her door. I waved at the two men and climbed into my seat beside her.

"What next?" Veronica asked as she pulled out of the lot.

I was surprised she didn't have a plan.

"We need to talk to Jacqui and to Cory," I said. "Why don't you go see Jacqui sometime before school is out today, so Parker won't be home. And after school's out, I'll see if I can track down Cory."

"I'll go over to Jacqui's after I drop you back at church," she said. "I'll go on the pretense of checking in on how she's doing, but I'll see what I can find out about where she was on Saturday and what's wrong with her car."

We hadn't been gone long, but when I returned to the office, Pastor Coker was pacing.

"Beckett!" He put his hand on his heart. "I was about to call the police."

Whoops. Veronica and I hadn't thought to tell anyone where we were going.

He continued, "Your car was in the lot, but I couldn't find you. And Veronica left without telling me. I didn't know what had happened!" He plopped down into one of the chairs by my desk and breathed deeply.

"I'm so sorry, Pastor Coker. We weren't thinking. Veronica and I went to visit Suzanne."

He sat up straight. "You did?"

I told him enough to keep him from being too curious, but I didn't tell him everything. I'd let Veronica decide how much she wanted to tell him. He wouldn't be happy to know she was on her way to visit a potential murderer. I sucked in a deep breath. I shouldn't have let her visit Jacqui alone. What were we thinking?

Pastor Coker must have seen the panic on my face. "What's wrong?"

"Uh, I remembered I need to run a couple of errands. I forgot to go to the bank yesterday, and I need to stop somewhere else really quick."

He wouldn't care about the late deposit, so it was a good excuse to get out of the office and check on Veronica.

"Take your time. Greg is subbing at the high school today, but I'll be here to answer the phone. Let me grab the money for you."

He heaved himself out of the chair and retrieved the bank envelope from the office safe. I stuffed the envelope into the bottom of my purse for safekeeping, as I wasn't intending to stop at the bank first.

I made it to Jacqui's house in record time, but then I wasn't sure what to do. Sit in my car and watch for something suspicious to happen? Sneak up to the window and peek in? Go in? I inched by and craned my neck to see if I anyone was visible inside. No, Jacqui had sheer curtains at the living room window.

I circled the block and pulled in by the curb a few houses down from Jacqui's. I turned off the engine and drummed my fingers on the steering wheel. A knock sounded on the passenger window, and I jumped in my seat. Aunt Starla waved at me and tried to open the door, but it was locked. I typically never locked my doors, but things were different this week. I leaned across the seat to roll down the window.

"What are you doing here?" we asked each other.

"You first," she said.

I hastily explained what was happening.

"You'd better get in there." She unlocked the door, opened it, cranked the window back up, relocked it, and slammed it shut in the time it took me to get out.

"Why are you here?" I asked.

She pointed at the house I had parked in front of. A lady was on her knees in a flower bed to the side of it. "This is the house I'm helping with. Now, go on. And fill me in when you come back out."

I hurried across the street and up Jacqui's sidewalk. I paused before ringing the doorbell, as I hadn't considered what I was going to say. Jacqui appeared on the other side of the glass storm door before I could work it out.

"It's like a First Comm reunion," she said as she let me in.

I pretended to be surprised to see Veronica, even though her car was in the drive. When Jacqui wasn't looking, she mouthed, "What are you doing here?" I ignored her and joined her on the red-and-blue plaid couch, across the coffee table from Jacqui on a matching love seat.

"I wanted to check in on you today," I said, "and see if you need anything. Though Mrs. Coker probably has that all taken care of."

"We were talking about how this all happened," Veronica said pointedly. "I was telling her I'm certain her mother has been framed."

"Oh! Do you think so?" I asked. "Hmm. Well, that makes sense. I can't believe Suzanne would even think about killing anyone, much less do it."

I hoped my voice sounded natural, but Jacqui was looking at me skeptically. I wasn't a great actor. She looked back and forth between Veronica and me a few times.

"What gives, ladies?" Jacqui asked. No beating around the bush for her. She was more like her mother than she would ever admit.

"Okay, fine," Veronica conceded. "The two of us were talking this morning about how we think somebody set your mother up, so we thought we'd see if you had any ideas. I guess we got our wires crossed about who was going to come by."

Jacqui seemed to buy her explanation, and I released the breath I hadn't realized I'd been holding.

I said, "The problem is so many people could have killed Aidan." She didn't need to know our suspect list held only three names. "Anyone could have snuck into the church kitchen and done it."

"Lots of people can prove where they were at the time, though," Jacqui said. "And some of those people were at the church." She focused her gaze on me. "We know for certain you were there." She turned to Veronica. "And where were you?"

Veronica turned her face away from Jacqui, "I had gone home from the reception to grab a sweater."

Jacqui pointed at her. "Since you live next door to the church, you were technically there too."

This conversation was not going the way we had planned.

Jacqui continued, "How do I know it wasn't one of you? This ..." she waved her hand back and forth between us, "... whatever it is ... could be your way of taking the focus off yourselves."

Veronica was not going to stand for Jacqui's accusation. "Where were *you* Saturday afternoon, young lady?"

"I was right here at home with Parker. You can ask him when he gets home from school."

Veronica stood and tapped my shoulder. "There's no need for that. Let's go, Beckett."

She marched out and I scurried after her. Jacqui slammed the door behind us.

"Well, I never!" Veronica said and then speared me with her eyes across the top of her car. "Why did you show up? Things were going fine until you arrived."

I checked to make sure the house door was still shut

and lowered my voice. "Because I realized I sent you to the home of a potential murderer all by yourself!"

Her shoulders fell. "You're right. I didn't think about that either." She looked me in the eye. "Thank you."

I glanced at the house again. "Let's get out of here and talk somewhere else. I've got an errand to run but can meet you back at the church in fifteen minutes or so."

"Great." She started to get into the car but then stepped back out. "Is Harold in the office?"

"Yes."

"Then let's meet at The Check instead."

I gave Veronica a thumbs up and hurried back to my car. Aunt Star was no longer in sight, so I decided to catch up with her later.

It was my mother's day to work at the bank, so the drive-thru was not an option. Going inside to her teller window would result in a lecture about forgetting the church deposit, but I'd get a bigger lecture if I used the drive-thru and she found out about it. So I parked my car at the church and crossed the street to the bank.

When I placed the fat envelope in front of Mom, she pursed her lips but said nothing. While she counted the cash and added up the checks, I wandered around the lobby. I grabbed a Tootsie Roll from the crystal dish on the table inside the front door, unwrapped it, and popped it in my mouth.

I inwardly cursed my sweet tooth when the bank's president, Mr. Adamson, called out a hello to me. I tried to quickly chew and swallow the candy, but I choked and started coughing. He raced out of his office and pounded his fist on my back, almost knocking me over. I finally stopped coughing and sucked in a deep breath. Mr. Adamson guided me to a plush armchair in the center of the lobby.

"Stay there," he said. "I'll go get you a glass of water."

My choking episode had drawn the attention of everyone in the bank, but once they realized I wasn't going to die in front of them, they returned to their business. I couldn't help but notice my mother didn't come check on me. She was still adding up checks.

Mr. Adamson returned with the water, and I drank it dutifully while he stood over me. When I finished, I handed the glass back to him, thanked him, and headed back to Mom's window.

"That was quite the performance," she said.

"I didn't do it on purpose."

"Mm-hm. It distracted me so I had to start over."

"Sorry."

This time I stood and waited in silence as she

finished the transaction. When I left, I headed down the street to The Check. I felt a twinge of guilt for leaving Pastor Coker in charge of the office, but it had been his wife's idea to meet elsewhere.

A quick scan of the diner revealed Callie wasn't working. I slid into the booth across from Veronica. She leaned toward me and started speaking before I was even settled.

"Being home alone with your young child doesn't count as an alibi," she said.

"Exactly."

"She could have gotten to church, done the deed, and been back home in ten minutes. He maybe wouldn't even have noticed she was gone."

While the waitress was taking our order, I thought for a moment. Something wasn't adding up.

I said, "Here's the thing, though. How would Jacqui have known Aidan would be alone and in the kitchen at that exact minute? For that matter, how would Cory know? How would anyone who wasn't at the church know he was off by himself when he was?" I tapped my chin. "This had to have been a spur-of-the-moment killing, don't you think? You wouldn't plan something like this out in the hopes you'd arrive at the right time to catch him alone."

Veronica sat back. "That does take Jacqui out of the

picture," she said. "She wouldn't have even known how long anyone would be there. Cory, on the other hand, would have had an idea of what was happening at the church, since he was across the street."

"Right. Maybe Aidan came outside, and Cory lured him back in. Or Cory might have gone inside and somehow got Aidan alone."

"Get your list back out," Veronica said. "We may have crossed some others off too soon."

I dug the notebook out of my purse and opened it to the "Suspects" page. For a moment I reflected on the fact that Veronica and I were working together on this and not getting on each other's nerves.

Veronica turned the notebook toward herself and pulled a pen out of her own purse. Perhaps we were irritating each other a little. She put a question mark after Jacqui's name.

Then she said, "What we need to do is make a new list and include everyone who was at the church at the time or who had a view of the church."

"That would include Suzanne, you know."

"Yes, I realize that. It would also include you, as Jacqui so eloquently stated."

"And you," I added.

She nodded. "We need to be thorough."

Before she could start her new list, a squeal of tires

followed by metal crashing against metal sounded in the near distance.

FIFTEEN

OUR ATTENTION TURNED toward the windows, where nothing appeared to be out of the ordinary. Within seconds, everyone in the diner ran to the door simultaneously. My bad leg left me at the back of the pack.

More tire squealing echoed from beyond the church, and the vehicle headed away from us. We all raced across the street and around the corner of the church on to Oak Street. No cars were in sight.

"There it is!" someone at the front of the group yelled, but I was too far behind to see. Other people had streamed out of businesses on Main and Oak, and most of them were faster than me. When I rounded the church into the parking lot and pushed my way through the crowd, I gasped. My car had been completely smashed in on the driver's side.

A woman yelled, "Somebody call the police!"

"I'll do it," Mr. Adamson said as he scuttled back across the street to the bank. I wondered if anyone had stayed behind to guard the money.

My mother marched toward the car. "This is unbelievable!"

"Don't touch it!" I ordered.

Mom stopped in her tracks and turned to me. "Whyever not?"

I tried not to be hurt that she was questioning me instead of hugging me.

Veronica stepped forward and put her arm around my shoulder. "Let's allow the police to investigate this before we disturb anything. Everyone step back from the car." She gave me a slight squeeze before letting go and herding us all to the picnic tables at the end of the lot. A few people reluctantly left to go back and attend to their unlocked businesses.

I took a seat facing outward at one of the tables. My mother sat next to me and gave me a squeeze. "You good?" she asked.

I shrugged and sighed. "Why would someone do this?"

She pursed her lips. "Have you been trying to find out who killed Aidan, even though I told you not to *and* someone has been arrested for it?"

"Yeeeees."

"Then I'm thinking that person might be after you too. I warned you about this!"

Pastor Coker had joined the crowd and sat to my

other side. Veronica marched up and made him slide down so she could sit by me.

"Why would they smash my empty car, though?" I asked them. "If they wanted to hurt me, they should have done it with me *in* the car."

Veronica said, "This way they could scare you off, but without the fear of you recognizing them."

I held a finger up, climbed onto the bench, and addressed everyone. "Did any of you see the car that did this?"

A few people shook their heads or said no. Then all our heads turned as two police cruisers pulled into the other end of the lot and parked along the far edge. Darren, Mitchell, and Frank stepped out. Mitchell's eyes scanned the crowd. He spotted me and raised his hand in greeting. I briefly waved back and tried not to blush. I didn't need my mother asking questions.

Mitchell and Frank walked over to inspect the scene while Darren made his way across the lot to us.

"Beckett," he said and nodded his head off to the side, "will you step over here with me, please?"

Pastor Coker helped me down from my perch atop the bench.

"Mrs. Coker, I need you as well," he added.

"I guess you need me, too, since I was right here in the building," Pastor Coker said.

"No, I just need the ladies for now." Darren turned and strode away.

I turned to Veronica, who held her palms up. She knew no more than I did. We followed Darren until he stopped out of earshot of the rest of the onlookers.

"We will talk about this," he swept his hand in the direction of my car, "in a minute. First, you should know Jacqui Storm called the police department a little while ago."

I tried and failed not to glance at Veronica, who was stoically focused on Darren.

He continued, "She wanted to file a complaint against you two. She said you came to her house and accused her of murder."

"We did not!" I declared.

Veronica's hands balled into fists. "That little ..." She pressed her lips together.

Darren crossed his arms. "Would you like to tell me what happened?"

Veronica and I turned to each other. She nodded at me.

I took a deep breath. "We went by to check on her. You know, since you've arrested her mother for murder. While we were there, we may have asked her where she was at the time Aidan died."

Darren sighed.

"She suggested we each could have done it too!" Veronica exclaimed.

I nodded. "And she did that before we asked where *she* was on Saturday afternoon. She was harassing *us!*"I jabbed my finger so hard into my chest I started coughing.

Veronica patted me on the back.

Darren shook his head. "You two," he pointed at each of us in turn, "need to stop looking for Aidan's murderer. We've charged someone."

"Yes," I said, "but—"

He held up his hand. "No 'buts,' Beckett. Stop investigating." He cleared his throat. "Let me go see what Frank and Mitchell have to say. Wait here."

The three men chatted for a few moments. Then Frank pointed to a few areas on the car and the pavement, and they inspected some bushes along the side of the church.

Darren crossed back to us while Mitchell and Frank went to address the rest of the crowd, which had grown over the past few minutes.

"Why were you looking in the bushes?" I asked.

"When Frank was inspecting the wider area, he noticed some of the bushes had a few broken branches. He thought a piece of debris from the crash might have flown over there, but we saw nothing but a few fresh footprints in the dirt."

"Weird," I said.

"At least irrelevant," Darren replied.

"What about Beckett's car?" Veronica asked.

"It does appear to be deliberate. There are tire marks where a vehicle sped up rapidly and did not slow down as it approached the car." He swept his arm toward the street. "We found more tire tracks where they peeled out of the parking lot. Did none of you see who did it?"

"We were at The Check. And nobody over there would admit to seeing anything." I waved my hand to the ever-growing crowd talking to the other officers.

Veronica added, "A few people did leave before Beckett asked."

"Really? People left before finding out what happened? In Cherry Hill?" Darren asked with a smirk.

"Crazy, right?" I grinned. "I think they were all people who had left their shops empty and unlocked."

Darren took down a list of their names so he could follow up with them later. He then asked for our version of events, which didn't take long.

I asked, "Was there enough time between when Jacqui called the police station and when this happened that it could have been her?"

Darren's lips formed a straight line, and he closed his eyes for a few seconds before he spoke. "Beckett Monahan, I am warning you one last time—"

I put a hand up. "I get it. No more private investigating for me." He couldn't see I had crossed the fingers of my other hand behind my back. I didn't like lying, but I couldn't let this go.

He begrudgingly added, "But we will check Jacqui's car. Considering what your car looks like, the other vehicle will have some front-end damage."

I looked at my car and shook my head. Driving it home from work would not be an option. In fact, I wasn't sure anyone would ever drive my car again. It wasn't worth much, so I had little doubt the insurance company would total it.

———

THE REST OF the workday was busy. The church phone rang continuously, both with people asking about the crash and about the funeral arrangements. Veronica and I didn't get another chance to put our heads together about the suspects, and I didn't even have time to think about it. Nor did I have time to talk to Cory after school.

Aidan's funeral visitation was that night from 6:00–

9:00 at Coopers' Funeral Home. My parents were picking me up at 5:40 to get in line early.

I didn't like going to visitations alone, because you never knew who you'd get stuck next to in line that you'd have to talk to while waiting. It was good to have someone built in for conversation. I also didn't have a working car at the moment. My smashed-up car had been towed to the salvage lot, and Pastor Coker had given me a ride home.

When you live in a small town, you go to a lot of funeral visitations because you know almost everyone. When you work at a church, you go to even more funerals than the typical resident.

Over the nearly two years I'd been back in Cherry Hill, I had amassed a small collection of "funeral dresses." A few were all black—those were reserved for the actual funerals. The others were mostly black, but they also had a pop of color, because I can't help myself. Those dresses were earmarked for visitations where the atmosphere would be expected to be almost jovial, like if the newly departed had lived a good, long life.

I didn't anticipate Aidan's visitation to be anything near jovial, given his age and the circumstances surrounding his death, so I put on one of the long-sleeved black dresses and slipped into some black pumps. My curls were disorderly, so I corralled them in a banana clip covered with black satin.

A car horn sounded out front, and I raced down the stairs, grabbed my black jacket, and headed out the door. After I slid into my parents' car, I realized I hadn't changed out the dangly red earrings I'd worn to work. With my hair pulled back, they would be on full display.

Dad had already taken off down the street, though, and I wouldn't be able to convince him to turn around. I considered whether to leave the earrings in or go without. After fiddling with them for a few seconds I left them in. I decided Aidan would have liked them.

"Have you heard from Aunt Star?" I asked. "I haven't seen or heard from her since this morning."

Mom said, "She's meeting us there. She had a late meeting at the office."

I was glad she wouldn't be going alone.

Though we arrived early, the small parking lot was jammed, and the line was close to snaking out the door. Dad took our jackets to the coat room as Mom and I joined the line behind a couple near my parents' age. They began chatting, which left me to fend for myself against the next arrivals. The outside door opened, and I held my breath until Trixie and Scott walked through. I exhaled with a smile.

"Sorry you have to do this on your birthday," I said. "I didn't expect to see you here, though. You didn't know Aidan all that well."

She pointed to her husband. "He plays—played—basketball with Aidan on Saturday mornings."

"Along with the rest of the town, so it seems."

She looked confused, but instead of commenting, she asked about the crash.

The line grew longer behind us, and as the door to the viewing room opened at six o'clock, Aunt Star rushed in and joined us. She reached up and touched my hair, and I batted her hand away.

"Get your hands off my banana clip! If you touch it, it'll start slipping loose."

"Sorry," she replied. "A wild curl is sticking out funny."

"Okay, but be very careful," I said.

She exaggeratedly fixed my hair. Then she slipped out of her jacket, straightened her dress, and smoothed her own hair. She was as stylish as ever, and she was born to wear black. The color washed out my complexion, which was another reason I liked adding bright colors to my outfits.

"Nice earrings," she said.

I reached up and touched them as we moved into the viewing room.

She added, "Aidan would have appreciated the color, I think."

I smiled and gave her arm a squeeze.

She checked to make sure my parents weren't paying attention and then whispered, "I heard about your car. You need to stop trying to solve this murder. We don't need another death on our hands—especially not yours."

I whispered back, "But they're already after me. They won't know if I've stopped or not. I have to keep going until I catch them."

Trixie poked me in the back. "What are you two whispering about?"

We turned to include her in our conversation.

Aunt Star said in a low voice, "I'm trying to get her to stop her quest to figure out who killed Aidan before she gets killed herself."

"Yes," Trixie said, "but if the murderer is on to her, wouldn't it make more sense to figure it out instead of quitting?"

I faced my aunt and crossed my arms. "Exactly."

She held both hands up. "Okay, okay, but don't you dare go anywhere or do any investigating on your own. Take someone with you."

"Like Mitchell," Trixie said with a grin.

I rolled my eyes at her.

Mom leaned toward us and said, "Girls, stop your gossiping or whatever and pay attention. We're almost to the family."

I rolled my eyes again but straightened my dress and prepared to talk to Aidan's family. I was glad my aunt was there to greet people with me and help keep the conversation going if we got held up with one family member for a while. That situation was always awkward if you didn't know the person well.

We spoke to Aidan's parents and then reached Shane and Blair. Aunt Star hugged Shane, while Blair clung to me like we were twins who'd been separated at birth.

"Isn't this so awful?" she said. "I can hardly bear it." She released the embrace but grabbed my shoulders and brought her face uncomfortably close to mine. "I want to apologize for the other day. I wasn't thinking straight, but who would be?" she babbled on. "It's so crazy. Aidan and I weren't close, but he was my brother-in-law—for about a half hour! Shane is distraught, as you could guess."

I extricated myself from Blair's grasp and stole a glance at the man in question, who was deep in conversation with Aunt Star. He didn't seem to be broken up to me, but he might be a master at keeping his emotions in check.

Blair continued, "After this mess is all over, I'd love it if we could be friends. Do you think we could?"

I blinked a few times and stammered out, "I g-guess so."

She embraced me again. "That's so great. I'll call you." She even held her hand to her face with her thumb and pinky extended like it was a phone receiver.

Normally that would have been the end of the conversation, but we were stuck in an awkward silence, since the line was stalled. I nudged my aunt and we switched places so she could talk to Blair while I chatted with Shane. Since I didn't know him well, I said the usual pleasantries.

Another man came up behind him and clapped a hand on his shoulder. Shane winced for a second before smoothing his face over and turning to the man.

The line then moved ahead, so we greeted a few more family members before finally viewing the body. This was always my least favorite part. You were expected to say something like, "He looks so lifelike," or, "They did such a good job with the makeup," or some other inane thing, which was bad enough. This time all I could think about was what he had looked like the last time I saw him. I suppressed a shiver.

Aunt Star grabbed my hand and squeezed so tightly I was sure she'd crack a bone. I then realized she was shaking, so I pulled my hand free, put my arm around her, and led her away from the casket. I pulled some tissues out of a conveniently located box and shoved them into her hand as I guided her to some wooden folding chairs along the wall.

We sat in silence for a few minutes while she composed herself. I took the opportunity to people watch. Marty James, the groomsman who had been in the kitchen with me and who managed the hardware store across from the church, was talking to Shane, who was now sitting on a stool instead of standing. I wondered why he hadn't gotten any seating for his new wife or his mom.

I switched my focus back to Marty, and I tried to remember if he had been in the church parking lot after the crash that afternoon. I closed my eyes to picture the scene but couldn't see him there, though almost everyone else who worked downtown had been in the crowd.

My eyes popped open. Marty was at the church on Saturday. He could be the man Greg had seen in the parking lot Friday night. He knew Suzanne. He could have easily slipped into the building to retrieve the bat, and he could have rammed my car. I wasn't sure about a motive, but a lot of people had one, so maybe he did too.

I excitedly whispered to my aunt, "I think I might know who did it!"

SIXTEEN

I HAD BARELY GOTTEN the words out when Cheryl Young Stouffer, a former classmate, sank into the chair on my other side. Cheryl was Aidan's cousin and the daughter of Barbara at the police station. She had also been the homecoming queen and president of our senior class. We exchanged some small talk and then started discussing our ten-year class reunion, which was planned for June.

Aunt Star started tearing tissues into strips. I wished she'd go talk to someone else instead of impatiently waiting for me. After about ten minutes, we finally broke away from Cheryl, but on our way out multiple other people stopped us, so we didn't get a chance to chat with each other. I also had to find my parents and tell them Aunt Star was taking me home.

When we eventually escaped the confines of the funeral home, I breathed a sigh of relief. Before I shared my theory, though, another conversational obstacle appeared: Darren.

"Starla. Beckett." He gave us a single nod. "You

ladies doing all right?" he asked.

I waited for Aunt Star to answer, but she only nodded.

"I'm as okay as I can be when my friend has been murdered and my car has been smashed in," I said.

He nodded again.

"Any idea who did it yet?" I asked.

"No. We've asked around at the local machine shops to see if anyone has brought in a vehicle with front-end damage, but no luck. The person probably figured we'd do that, though, so they'd be hiding the vehicle."

"That would make sense."

Aunt Star said, "Beckett was telling me—"

I interrupted her before she could continue. Though I didn't intend to keep my promise to not try to solve the murder, Darren didn't need to know that.

"Yes," I said loudly, "I was telling her how quickly you and the guys got to the church today. Thanks for that."

He gave me a calculated look and said, "No problem. Just down the street, you know."

I grabbed Aunt Star's hand and started to pull her down the sidewalk. "Great to see you, Darren. Talk to you later."

He stood and watched us speculatively as I tugged

my aunt along. She waved at him, and he raised a hand in return. He then shook his head and turned away.

"Why did you do that?" Aunt Star asked as she started the engine and pulled away from the curb.

"Do what?"

"Not let me tell Darren you think you know who killed Aidan. Who is it, by the way?"

"I promised him I'd stop investigating." I took a deep breath. "And I think Marty James might be the killer." I explained my reasoning.

She put her foot on the brake and made a left turn when she should have continued driving straight.

"Where are we going?"

"We're driving back by the funeral home to see if we can spot Marty's truck. When we left, he was talking to Edna."

The newspaper editor was quite chatty, so Marty might still be stuck there.

"You know," I said, "I bet that car *was* following us last night."

She looked at me but didn't say anything. I knew she was wishing she had told Darren about it.

We slowly drove down all the streets surrounding the funeral home while we kept our eyes peeled for Marty's black Chevy Silverado four-by-four. She then cruised through the parking lot. The truck was nowhere to be seen.

"Now what?" I asked. "His truck not being here doesn't prove anything. Maybe he already left or he rode with someone else."

"We'll do a drive-by of his house."

Marty lived a mile outside of town in a small, remodeled farmhouse. Since his divorce a few years earlier, he sometimes had a roommate. I wasn't sure if anyone else was living there now.

Aunt Star must have read my mind. "Kyle Korte has been living with him for a couple months," she said. "They might have ridden to the visitation together. I did see Kyle there."

She slowed the car as we approached Marty's house. His truck was not in his driveway, but something looked off about his place.

"Pull into the drive," I said.

Aunt Star hit the brakes and turned in.

"Why does this look different than normal?"

After a few seconds, my aunt said, "The shed doors are shut."

A large white metal shed stood about fifty feet beyond the house. I didn't think I'd ever seen the giant doors closed. They were always wide open, with the contents of the shed in full view for anyone who cared to look. Those contents weren't anything to write home about: stacks of wooden pallets, an ancient riding lawnmower, some metal barrels, and other odds and ends. It seemed to be a catchall for things Marty didn't want to get rid of.

"Drive back there," I said.

"Are you crazy?" she asked.

"We have to see if his truck is in there and check for damage."

"What if they come home? Or what if Marty's already home?" Aunt Star asked. I was surprised she wasn't gung-ho about my idea. She wasn't afraid of much.

"You'll think of something," I said. "If nothing else, you can flirt with them."

She turned off the lights and shifted the car into gear. "True."

We pulled to a stop outside the doors, and she left the car running while I jumped out. I slid my fingers between the two doors, grasped the edge of one, and pulled with all my might. It didn't budge. Aunt Star crunched across the gravel in her heels and faced me so she could push while I pulled.

"One, two, three!" she yelled.

We grunted and groaned and finally edged the door open enough to slip through. The shed smelled of oil and grass clippings. Outside there had been enough moonlight to see by, but inside I could barely make out the outline of Marty's truck.

"I'll be right back," Aunt Star said.

I carefully made my way around the truck while keeping one hand on it to try to avoid falling in the dark. I had almost made it to the front when I could suddenly see and almost tripped from the shock. Aunt Star quickly joined me, flashlight in hand.

We rounded the front of the vehicle together and I sighed in defeat. Marty's truck had a heavy-duty cattle bumper on the front. Even if he had rammed my car, his vehicle wouldn't have much, if any, damage. In fact, it seemed perfectly fine to me. Aunt Star leaned closer and scratched at the bumper with her fingernail.

"There's something beige here," she said. She aimed the flashlight directly on her nail and then leaned down and sniffed it. She groaned. "Bird poop."

I had to work hard to not gag.

Too late we registered the sound of metal scraping against metal, and a light shone in our eyes. My heart began racing.

"What's going on out here?" Marty demanded.

I blinked a few times. "Uhhhh ..."

My aunt glided around me much more gracefully than I could have done in heels on an uneven dirt floor.

"I was thinking about getting a truck," she said while striding toward him, "and I wanted to check yours out."

"Uh-huh," he said with a heavy dose of skepticism.

I frantically looked around for something to use as a weapon if needed. I spotted a rifle hanging on the gun rack in the back window of Marty's truck, but he'd be able to grab it before I could. Not that I'd know how to use it anyway. A crowbar sat on the seat of the lawnmower, but again, Marty could reach it much faster than me.

"I like your bumper," my aunt said. "Where'd you buy it?"

She lightly touched Marty's arm. His stance became more rigid, but his focus remained on her.

Meanwhile, behind her back, she was using her other arm to shoo me toward the door. I tried to scurry around the other side of the truck without drawing his attention, but in the semi-darkness I tripped on a rock and stumbled into a metal barrel. Unfortunately, it was empty, so it turned over and into the barrel behind it with a crash, and I went with it.

I froze and squeezed my eyes shut, as if that would help anything. I opened them to discover Marty kneeling beside me and shining his flashlight up and down my body. He placed a hand on my shoulder, and

I tensed under his touch.

"Becky, are you hurt?" He had a concerned look in his eyes.

Aunt Star crouched beside him and asked, "Can you move everything? Is anything broken?"

I carefully rolled to my back with their help and then moved my arms and legs to test them out. I flexed my fingers and bent my knees.

"I think I'm fine," I said as I struggled to sit up.

They got on either side of me and guided me to my feet. When they let go, I wobbled a bit, and before I realized it Marty had swept me up into his arms. He strode out of the shed and deposited me into the passenger seat. He then put his hand on the top of the car and leaned down to look at me and Aunt Star, who had slipped into the driver's seat.

"I can guess why you ladies were *really* out here checking out my truck, and I'm not happy with the insinuation." Marty's eyes moved between Aunt Star and me. "This has been an emotional night for everyone, though, so why don't we forget this episode ever happened?"

We agreed, apologized, and were soon on our way up the driveway.

"Soooo maybe he's not the killer?" I said.

"You think?" Aunt Star pulled onto the highway

and stepped on the gas.

"Maybe I shouldn't have jumped the gun on someone who doesn't have an obvious motive."

"I've asked you this a lot lately," she said, "but are you okay?"

I rolled my head in a circle and stretched my arms out in front of me to test them. "I think so, but I bet my whole body will ache tomorrow."

"Speaking of tomorrow, are you planning to go to the funeral?" she asked.

"Yes, the whole church staff is going, even though Veronica is still extremely annoyed they're not holding the funeral at the church. You want to ride together?"

By the time we returned home we had come up with a plan for the next day. Transportation would be tricky until I could buy a new car. That couldn't happen until the insurance money came through.

The phone was ringing when we entered the house, and I grabbed it before it stopped. I answered and then held the receiver out to Aunt Star.

"Darren." I grinned at her and headed upstairs to change out of my dress.

When I emerged from my room a few minutes later, Aunt Star was coming down the hall from her own room. While I was now in my palm-tree pajamas, she had changed into jeans and a sweater.

"Going somewhere?"

"Darren's," was all she said as she started down the stairs.

I followed her. "Aha. Don't do anything I wouldn't do."

"Don't stay up." She grabbed her jacket and purse and hurried out the door into the garage.

I poured a bowl of chips, filled a glass with water, and was about to turn on the TV when I thought better of it and grabbed my notebook out of my purse instead. Suzanne was still in jail, and someone was definitely after me, so this murder needed to be solved.

As I settled into my place on the couch, the reality that a murderer was out to get me fully hit me. Not only that, but I was home alone, and I had no form of transportation, leaving me feeling vulnerable and exposed. I jumped up and closed the curtains on the picture window across from me.

Then I checked the locks on all the doors and first floor windows. The window over the kitchen sink was unlocked, which wasn't uncommon, as you had to close the window just right for the lock to turn.

I opened the window, slammed it shut, and held it down with one hand while turning the lock with the other. It didn't quite latch, so I tried again. I was successful on the third try. The lack of curtains unnerved me, but I took a deep breath and turned away from the window.

I needed someone to talk through the list of suspects with me, but it was too late to call Veronica without her husband wondering what we were up to. Trixie would be putting the kids to bed. She probably had better things to do on her birthday night anyway, especially after having to spend an hour of her evening at the funeral home.

With my mind more at ease about my safety, I returned to the couch, propped my feet on the coffee table, and opened my notebook to a fresh page. I chewed the end of my pen while I considered where to start. Then I got back up and fished a copy of the wedding program out of my purse. Most of the names were already there, so I would add to it.

I wrote Cory's name in the margin. I thought about who else would have had a good view of the church, and I added Callie's name, as well as Minnie Jensen, who had been at the washateria at the same time as Suzanne. I finished up with the names of a few other people who worked on Main and Oak Streets.

The list contained more than thirty names. I needed to eliminate some of them. First, I crossed off Blair's name. She never left the sanctuary. Then I scratched out Aidan's parents and his one living grandparent, as they had left for the reception directly after their family photos, and I couldn't imagine any of the three of them were capable of killing him.

I sighed when I realized the bridesmaids' and groomsmen's spouses or dates weren't on the list. It seemed like a losing cause. I gave the paper a fling, and it twirled across the room like a frisbee before landing on the floor by the front door.

Getting rid of the paper hadn't stopped my thoughts, so I got up to retrieve it. I reached down to grab it and heard a slight squeaking sound outside the door.

My heart momentarily stopped. I froze mid-crouch and held my breath, listening intently. After a few seconds I stood and flipped off the overhead light.

I gave my eyes time to adjust to the darkness and tiptoed over to the window to peek between the curtains. All was still and quiet out front. The noise hadn't come out of nowhere, though, and I wouldn't rest until I discovered what it was.

I let the curtains fall back together, and I stood in the dark for a minute before moving. I crossed back to the door, turned the lock, and slowly opened it a crack. The moonlight illuminated a white paper on the glass storm door.

As quickly as possible, I opened the door, pushed open the storm door, reached around and grabbed the note taped there, slammed both doors shut, and locked the interior one. I pressed my back against the door and slid to the floor, shaking.

When my breathing and heart rate returned to normal, I crawled over to the couch. I couldn't explain why I crawled, since nobody could have seen me, but it seemed like the thing to do. I climbed onto the couch and turned on the lamp on the side table. It cast a rosy glow through the mauve lampshade. The lamp was more decor than light source, but it gave out enough light to read the note I still grasped in my hand.

In red ink and all capital letters, the note read: "THIS IS YOUR LAST WARNING."

SEVENTEEN

I BEGAN SHAKING AGAIN. This is my last warning ... or what? I wondered. *Or what?*

All my senses were on high alert. I flipped the lamp back off and sat tensely perched on the edge of the couch in the darkness. The refrigerator's motor kicked on and I shrieked.

The person who had left the note had been in my front yard minutes earlier. If I hadn't closed the curtains, they would have been able to see me in all my palm-tree-pajama glory, yet I would have had no idea they were out there. I shuddered at the thought and made a mental note to always close the curtains from here on out.

I took a deep breath in through my nose and when I blew the air back out through my mouth, I relaxed all my muscles. The tension seeped out of me, and I knew I had a choice to make. I could go upstairs, get into bed, and try—and ultimately fail—to forget any of this had happened. Or I could do something about it. I could figure out who killed Aidan and get them put behind bars where they couldn't frighten me or anyone else ever again—at least not anyone who wasn't also in prison.

Once again, I turned on the lamp. I smoothed the note out on the coffee table and stared at it. The bold, slanted letters looked like a man's handwriting. Of course, a woman could have tried to disguise her handwriting, but the letters had been written confidently, not haltingly, as they would have been if someone wasn't used to writing that way.

I walked back over to the front door to finally retrieve the wedding program. While I was there, I turned the overhead light back on. The bright light made me blink and helped energize and motivate me. I crossed back to the couch and looked at the list. I pulled open the drawer on the end table and rifled through the contents until I found a pencil. It would be easier to erase a line than to have to make a new list if I changed my mind.

First, I crossed off anyone who was not from Cherry Hill. None of them would know Suzanne, and they wouldn't know where I live. Since the phone was in Aunt Starla's name, they wouldn't even be able to find me in the phone book.

Next, I crossed off all the remaining women. The handwriting looked like a man's, and none of the women had a decent motive.

Four names remained on the list: Cory Hankins, Marty James, Aidan's cousin Zane, and the groom, Shane Patrick. I scratched off Marty's name. After our encounter, I was pretty sure it wasn't him. I didn't know enough about Zane to know if he would have a motive or not. Surely I would have heard about it by now if he did. I drew a light line through his name.

I tapped my pencil on Cory's name a few times. I wished I'd had time to try to talk to him that afternoon. I looked at the clock on the living room wall. It was too late now to call his house. And what would I say even if I did call?

However, it might not be too late to call Greg. He had spent the day subbing at the school, so maybe he had talked to Cory. If I called Greg, I knew I was taking a chance he would take it as evidence I was interested in him, but I was willing to take that chance.

The problem with making a phone call was the phone was in the kitchen along with the curtainless window, and the phone cord wasn't long enough to stretch to the living room. Once again, I wished for a phone in my bedroom. The bedroom—that was it! I could use the phone in Aunt Star's room.

I grabbed my pencil and list and raced up the stairs and into her room, where I quickly closed the curtains before turning on the bedside lamp. I sank to the edge of the bed and picked up the receiver before I realized I didn't know Greg's number. It was written on the pad next to the downstairs phone. My heart rate sped up until I remembered I could call the operator.

The phone was soon ringing. Greg answered, and a burst of laughter sounded in the background.

"You having a party over there?" I asked.

"Of sorts," he said. "I told the boys from church they could come over here after the visitation if they wanted. I thought they might want to be together instead of on their own tonight."

"That was thoughtful," I said. "Who all is there?"

He rattled off five names, including Cory's. I lay back on the bed in relief when I heard his name. If he had been at Greg's all evening, he couldn't have left a note on my door a half hour earlier.

"Ah, good. They've been there awhile, then?" I asked.

"Yeah, for an hour at least. You want to come join us?"

"No, I need to get to bed soon. Plus, I don't have any way to get there."

"That's right!" he said. "I heard about your car."

We talked about the incident for a few minutes and when we started to say goodbye, he asked, "So did you call for any particular reason?"

I had to think quickly. Since I had my answer about Cory, I didn't want to mention my real reason to Greg. But if I said I had no real purpose for calling, he'd think I was interested in him.

"Um, well, I wanted to make sure you knew we're all going to the funeral tomorrow."

"Yes, Pastor Coker called to tell me. Thanks for checking," he said warmly.

"You're welcome. See you tomorrow!" I said brightly and hung up before he got the end of his goodbye out.

I sat back up and marked a decisive line through Cory's name.

Only one name remained: Shane Patrick. My heart sank. The pieces fit together perfectly, though I didn't want them to. Had I even subconsciously ignored his involvement in Suzanne's arrest? That would make him the obvious framer. His motive wasn't obvious, but many of the stories we'd heard about Aidan affected Shane or Blair in some way.

I flopped onto my back again and stared at the popcorn ceiling so long my eyes became unfocused, and the peaks turned into valleys. I shook my head to refocus and sat up.

What was I going to do? Should I call the police?

No, they'd tell me I was being silly and they already had their killer behind bars. Should I wait until morning to do my final investigating and confront Shane? I could, but I would run the risk he would have already left for the funeral home. I was not going to let him speak at Aidan's funeral if he was the killer.

I needed Aunt Star. Of all nights for her to be at Darren's. I could at least call over there and let her know about the note. Darren would take that seriously. She would almost certainly come home, but he might come with her. I wavered for a moment and then decided calling her was the best course of action.

My plan was not as easy as I thought it would be, however, because Darren's phone number was unlisted. That was a smart choice for a cop, but it was not so great for me.

All I could do was brave the kitchen and see if his number was written on the pad hanging by the phone. I carefully made my way back downstairs in the dark and crawled across the kitchen floor so nobody could see me unless their nose was to the glass on the curtainless window. Then I realized I couldn't see the numbers on the pad without the lights on, so I crawled back over to turn them on. All my work was to no avail, however, as Darren's number was nowhere to be found.

I sat back against the wall and dropped my head into my hands. A few seconds later, I quickly lifted my head. I got on my knees, reached up and grabbed the phone's handset, punched in the church's phone number, and dropped back down to the floor.

Pastor Coker answered sleepily on the fifth ring. "'Lo? Uh, First Comm."

"Hello. It's Beckett."

"Beckett, what's going on?" He suddenly sounded much perkier and quite concerned.

I hadn't counted on him answering, so I fumbled over my words for a moment. "Um, ah, I'm sorry to wake you," I said in what I hoped sounded like a weak and upset voice, "but can I talk to Mrs. Coker? I'm pretty worked up about Aidan. I need someone to talk to."

"Of course, honey. I'll wake her."

He must have put the phone down on the covers, because I could hear the two of them conversing, but the sound was muffled so I couldn't make out what they were saying. A minute later, Veronica greeted me.

"Mrs. Coker," I said in a much stronger voice than I had used with her husband, "I need to tell you—"

"Hold on," she said. "Harold, dear, if you're still there, you need to hang up. Now," she added firmly.

A click sounded on the line. I wondered how often they listened in on each other's phone conversations.

"I came down to the kitchen phone," she said. "You can talk freely now. He won't dare pick up again."

I filled her in on all the events of the evening, starting with our escapade at Marty's house.

"We have to do something now," I concluded. "This can't wait."

"You're right. It can't. Not only because we can't let him fake his way through the funeral, but also because Suzanne is still in jail, and she'll be there until someone else is arrested. She's in the real jail now. I heard that at the funeral home."

"Then we need to check out Shane's car," I declared.

"Are you sure?" she asked. "You've already gotten into a pickle once tonight doing that."

"That's where we have to start," I said. "We need a little more evidence before we confront him."

"Right," she said confidently. "Let's do it."

"Why don't you come over here? Tell Pastor Coker whatever you want. I don't care if you say I'm going into hysterics."

"I know how to handle him," she said. "Leave it with me. I'll be there in ten minutes."

"I'll be waiting. Don't come to the door until I flash

the porch light."

We hung up, and I needed to change my clothes. I was getting tired of crawling, and my body was starting to hurt from my earlier fall, so I heaved myself up and didn't look at the window as I rushed across the room.

Seven minutes later I descended the stairs wearing all black, but this time I was looking much more casual than earlier in the evening. I peeked out the curtains and spotted Veronica's car at the curb. I moved to the front door and flipped the porch light on and off.

A car door slammed, and I cracked the door open until Veronica appeared. I opened it a little wider, she slipped in, and I closed and locked the door behind her. I almost laughed when I took a good look at her. She was wearing a pair of black polyester pants and a giant black, hooded sweatshirt that obviously belonged to her husband.

She pointed a finger in my face and said, "Don't laugh. It's all I could come up with on short notice and without Harold asking what I was doing. I had to pull these out of the laundry in the basement."

Veronica turned and headed toward the kitchen, but I grabbed her arm. She arched an eyebrow at me, so I explained about the window. With a pointed look, she pulled her arm away and marched into the kitchen. I tentatively followed her and sat at the table with my back to the window. Veronica was facing it, daring any peeping toms to mess with her.

"You sure you want to do this?" I asked. "It could be dangerous."

She narrowed her eyes at me. "You think I don't realize that?"

"Your husband will never forgive me if something happens to you."

"First, I'm a big girl and can make my own decisions. Second, you know for a fact he would forgive you. That's the kind of man he is."

I nodded.

"He's also the kind of man who would pray in this situation, and that's what we're going to do."

I nodded again and bowed my head as she said a short but very precise prayer. She didn't so much ask but tell God what to do. I was fine with that.

EIGHTEEN

VERONICA AND I MADE a brief plan, grabbed two flashlights, and slipped out the back door. Shane and Blair's new house was a few blocks away. All we had to do was stay off the streets to keep from being seen and to avoid yards with dogs.

We made our way through one block of backyards and across one street without incident, but halfway through the next block I stumbled on a tree root and yelped. Veronica caught me before I fell, but the noise roused a dog, who began barking, leapt out of its doghouse, and lunged toward us. I stiffened, and Veronica clapped her hand over my mouth to keep me from screaming before I realized the dog was chained and couldn't get to us.

Lights came on in the house, so Veronica dragged me across the yard and behind the neighbor's house. She was surprisingly strong and nimble. She peeked around the corner and whispered a play-by-play of the homeowner opening the door and looking around. He yelled at the dog to settle down and retreated into the house. I let out a long breath.

Veronica flipped her hood up and motioned for me to follow her. Two yards later, we were next door to the Patricks' house, which spanned two lots. We crouched behind a bush to survey the area.

No lights shone from the windows of the two-story mock-Tudor style home, though a second story window was open. The backyard did not contain a doghouse, and I hoped no dog slept inside the house or garage. The detached three-car garage stood behind and a little to the side of the house. A covered walkway connected it to the house.

I had recovered from my fright with the dog, and I was ready to take charge again. I led Veronica across the small expanse of backyard to the garage. We crept along the side to the door under the walkway. I tried the knob, but it was locked, which was a little out of the ordinary in Cherry Hill. However, considering Shane drove a brand-new Ford F250 pickup, and Blair zipped around town in a little two-door Mercedes, they had good reason to lock up.

I prayed we'd find a window or two on the other side of the garage. We slipped around the corner to discover two double-hung windows with no screens. The first wouldn't budge, but the second slid up without a catch or a sound. I helped Veronica climb through and she returned the favor.

We pulled out our flashlights, but enough moonlight streamed through the windows that we didn't need them until we moved past Blair's coupe, which had no visible damage. Veronica then clicked her light on but kept it pointed at the floor.

The dim light revealed the cleanest, most organized garage I had ever seen. That was mostly because it was new, but the orderliness of the lawn-mowing equipment, sporting gear, tools, and assorted boxes was obvious. Everything had a place, which was helpful when you needed to not trip over anything in the dark.

Veronica flicked her light up and along the front bumper of Shane's pickup. It didn't have an additional guard of any kind, and it was in pristine shape. I couldn't decide if I was relieved or not.

The third garage stall held another vehicle covered with a tarp. I picked up the edge to take a peek, and the heavy canvas began to slide toward us. When the far edge slid over the top, it flipped over and knocked the flashlight out of Veronica's hand.

The large, metal light hit Shane's truck with a clang before falling to the floor. It then bounced, ricocheted off my ankle, and rolled under the truck, where it came to a stop, still shining. I shrieked and grabbed my ankle. Veronica shushed me.

She whispered, "I'm going to crawl under there and grab that light. You check this car for damage."

Veronica shoved the tarp to the side so she could get under the truck while I turned to the uncovered vehicle. Even without turning on my light, I could see the front end of the old, brown four-door Buick was not in perfect condition. I switched on my small plastic light and leaned over to inspect it more closely. I placed a hand on the car's massive steel hood to steady myself. It was cold to the touch.

The chrome grill had sustained some minor damage, and the hood ornament was crooked. Though the damage was superficial, I was almost certain this was the car that had crashed into mine. It would take a lot to make much of a dent in this car. My little Torino hadn't stood a chance.

Light filled the garage and a click sounded from underneath the pickup. I froze. Without moving, I glanced under the truck, where Veronica was lying on her side facing me. Her eyes were huge. She placed a shaky finger in front of her lips, and I quickly looked away. I stuck my flashlight back into the front pocket of my sweatshirt, as I didn't want to make a sound by turning it off.

"Who's there?" Shane asked.

He couldn't yet see me, because the truck was in the way and I was still hunched over, but it was only a matter of time. The garage had no hiding spots where Shane wouldn't instantly find me. However, he didn't need to know about Veronica. I said a split-second silent prayer, stood, and walked along the front of the pickup until he could see me.

"You," he said.

"Yes, me."

"I thought I gave you one last warning," he said menacingly as he stood in the doorway.

"You did." My heart was in my throat, but I needed to start coming up with more than two-word responses. "Why did you do this?"

He threw his head back and laughed. I took the opportunity to look around and see if there were any possible means of escape or any weapons close at hand. The window was still open, and it was closer to me than to him, but I'd never get there before Shane would. I also couldn't leave Veronica behind. The tools were also too far away to be helpful, but a barrel of sports equipment stood mere feet away. I inched toward it.

Shane stopped laughing maniacally, locked eyes with me, and took a few stumbling steps in my direction. He was drunk, which could complicate matters. I stopped moving.

"That man was the bane of my existence," he spat out. "He's always been nothing but trouble. I've been cleaning up his messes my entire life, even though I'm seven years younger."

He paused as if waiting for me to respond.

"I can see how hard that would be," I said.

"He never had to work for anything. Star of all the sports teams without even trying. He inherited the construction business when Uncle Stan died. What did I get? That stupid car!" He dramatically swept his arm toward the Buick. "Why would I want that car? But I couldn't sell it. My dad would have had a fit. 'It's a classic,' he says."

Shane took another step closer to me. He was now between Blair's car and his truck. I forced myself to not look down at where Veronica was lying a few feet away from him. I took a step back, but I wasn't quite close enough to reach the sports barrel.

"And the women—the *women*. So many of them. Anyone he wanted any time he wanted. Except your aunt, of course. She didn't always come running." He tipped his head to the side and chuckled. "I respect her for that." He nodded toward me. "But I bet if he'd told you to jump, you'd say, 'How high?'"

I couldn't deny it. The man had possessed an animal

magnetism. Shane doubled over in laughter, and I prayed he wouldn't lean over far enough to see Veronica. I took another step backward, bumped into the barrel, and reached behind me to grab the edge.

If he would only take one more step toward me, that might give Veronica enough room to scoot out behind the truck and escape through the open doorway without him noticing.

"B-but why did you do it at your wedding?" I asked. "Why ruin that day for Blair?"

"Blair, Blair, Blair. Everything's about Blair. Or Aidan. Not him anymore, though—not after tomorrow. The funeral is bound to be insufferable with everyone saying good things about him, as if he was perfect. He wasn't. He *wasn't!*" Shane punched a finger into the air.

Then he pointed that finger at me. "Do you want to know the final straw? Do you?" He paused for me to answer what I had assumed was a rhetorical question.

"I do."

"After the rehearsal, I saw him whispering in Blair's ear. And she smiled. *She smiled.* The man was hitting on my fiancée the night before my wedding. I followed him out to his truck and told him to stay away from her. What did he do? He laughed at me. Said I was crazy." He jabbed his finger into his chest.

"Me!"

That explained the encounter in the parking lot, but I had one more question.

"Why did you bring Suzanne into it?"

He smiled. "That was perfect. While you were off trying to find Aidan at the church, I looked out the window and saw Suzanne at the washateria. Didn't think anything of it at the time, but later I realized I could frame her." He cackled. "It was so easy—even easier than sneaking up on Aidan in the church."

Shane started to take another stumbling step toward me but then changed his mind and turned to look into his truck bed. He reached an arm over and grabbed for an object I couldn't see.

With the hand behind me, I groped around in the barrel until my fingers closed around a hard, wooden, and cylindrical object—a baseball bat. I now had to turn to pull it out, but I was confident enough it would be a good weapon that I took my chance. My back was only turned for a few seconds, but when I faced Shane again, he was holding a crowbar in one hand and tapping it on to his other hand.

"What'cha got there, Becky?"

I grasped the bat with both hands and held it out in front of me like a sword.

"A bat."

Shane leered at me. "That's not *a* bat, Becky. That's *the* bat."

My eyes widened, and my gaze flickered to the bat. I almost dropped it, but then I gripped the barrel even more securely.

He rested the end of the crowbar against his shoulder.

"Ah, she figured it out," he said. "Aidan might have been the home-run hitter, but I'm the one who hit the grand slam—right into his skull."

He smiled fondly at the memory, and I tightened my grip on the bat.

"He went down with such a satisfying thump. Even hit his head again on the way down. Maybe you'll do the same."

Shane cackled, took another step toward me, and twirled the crowbar in a lazy circle in front of him. I chanced a glance at Veronica, who was kneeling under the truck just beyond him, holding her flashlight like ... well, a baseball bat.

I jerked my eyes back to Shane. He swayed and placed his free hand on the truck to support himself. He was now less than ten feet away from me. If Veronica and I were going to make our move, this was the time.

"Did you truly think you were going to get away

with it?" I asked. "Surely you knew that in *one* or *two* or *three* days," I took a quick look at Veronica, who nodded, "you'd be caught."

He looked at me quizzically. "What?"

"One, two, three!" I yelled.

Veronica swung the flashlight out and up from under the truck with all her might and hit Shane in the back of his left knee. His leg buckled, and he stumbled forward, swinging recklessly with the crowbar. He caught me in the hip before I could jump away or swing the bat at him.

Shane steadied himself and spun toward Veronica on his good leg. She had scrambled to her feet but had lost her grip on the flashlight, so she faced him with no weapon.

As he slowly reared back in preparation of taking a downward blow at her, I lurched forward and took a quicker swing of my own. The crowbar clattered onto the floor, and he roared in pain.

I leaned over to grab the crowbar and when I straightened back up, Darren, Mitchell, and Frank were stepping through the open door, guns drawn. I raised my hands and dropped the crowbar on the hood of Blair's car. The bat still hung from my other hand. I released it, and it bounced and rolled to Shane's feet.

We all froze in silence for a moment. Then Shane

grabbed his shoulder and jerked his head back and forth between me and Veronica. "They broke in here and attacked me in my own home! Arrest them both!"

"I don't think we'll be doing that," Darren said. "Looks a lot like self-defense to me."

He held his gun trained on Shane while Frank helped Veronica up and Mitchell cuffed Shane, who howled in pain. Darren then holstered his gun and opened the overhead door. Mitchell read Shane his rights as he marched him to the squad car.

I held the bat out to Darren. "Murder weapon."

His eyes lit up. "This is what you and Greg were talking about last night."

"Yep. You were so sure it was the rolling pin."

He hung his head and briefly closed his eyes. "Live and learn, I guess."

"I would have preferred to not have to face down a murderer with his own murder weapon in order for you to learn."

His lips twitched.

"Go ahead," I said. "Laugh if you want. Just know you're laughing at yourself."

He was still chuckling when Aunt Star's voice carried to us. "Can I come over there now?"

Darren waved her over, and she ran full tilt and nearly knocked me over in her rush to wrap her arms around me.

"Beckett Lee Monahan, you scared the living daylights out of me! Don't you ever do that again!"

I leaned my head back to look her in the eyes. "What? Catch a murderer?"

She rolled her eyes and squeezed me even more tightly.

NINETEEN

DESPITE THE LATE HOUR, Mitchell insisted that Veronica and I accompany them back to the station to give our statements. He explained that was the first step toward freeing Suzanne, so we went without too much grumbling.

Darren made the wise choice of not making Veronica ride in a police car. Aunt Star drove her, but since her car was a two-seater, that left me to ride shotgun with Mitchell.

I winced when I pulled the seatbelt across me. Mitchell must have been watching, because he asked if I was okay.

"I'm a little tender where the crowbar hit my hip," I said.

"What? He hit you? Why didn't you say? We should have gotten an ambulance."

"I'm fine, but I'll be sore for a few days. I also fell earlier tonight," I added, "and Veronica's flashlight hit my ankle on accident." Since I already had a limp, nobody had noticed I was walking a little strangely.

His eyes traveled up and down my body as he shook his head. "We'll get somebody to check you out at the station."

We rode in silence for about twenty seconds, but it seemed like an eternity.

"So, that guy Greg from last night ..." Mitchell trailed off and kept his eyes focused straight ahead.

I stifled a smile and hoped the darkness hid the blush creeping up my neck. "Yes?"

"Are you and he ... you know?"

"Dating?" I provided.

"That's the word."

"No."

After another few moments of silence, he said, "Good."

"Is it?" I asked.

"Yes." He glanced my way. "Do you think so?"

I pretended to think about my answer for a few seconds. "Yes."

He let out a small breath and repeated, "Good."

I wasn't sure if he was going to leave it at that, so I tried to prompt him. "So ..."

"Of course, you're currently a—"

I spluttered, "Surely I'm not a suspect anymore!"

"No. You're a witness."

"Oh."

"After I stuffed Shane into the squad car, he was so worked up he more or less confessed. We'll have to wait until he sobers up to get a confession we can rely on. If he does confess again, and then he pleads guilty in court, that means no trial, so no witnesses will be needed."

I nodded. "Got it. So this is a 'to be continued' situation."

"It is."

I allowed myself to smile this time. I cut my eyes toward Mitchell, who was grinning as well.

We pulled into the station and trooped in with everyone else. Frank led Shane through the door leading to the holding cells. Shane was past his belligerent stage and stumbled along sullenly.

Darren ushered Veronica and me into a small conference room I'd never seen before. He motioned for us to sit next to each other on one side of the table. He sat across from us, and a few seconds later Mitchell joined him.

Mitchell pressed the record button on a tape player and stated the date, time, and our names. He said, "We want to hear every detail of what happened tonight, but first I'd like you to explain how you came to suspect Shane of Aidan's murder."

Before that, I had a question I needed answered.

"We'll get to that, but how did you know to come to his house? We didn't tell anyone where we were going."

Darren explained, "Your aunt got home from ... uh, being out, and she saw Veronica's car out front, but neither of you were inside. She was understandably worried, and then she found the warning note, which led to her calling me at home."

He cleared his throat. "I rushed over, and by the time I got there, she had found the wedding program with your scribbles all over it. We realized it was a suspect list, and the only name not crossed off was Shane's. Starla told me about your adventure at Marty's, so we guessed you might be trying the same thing at Shane's house. I radioed the station, and you know the rest."

"I'm thankful she went home when she did," I said. "She must have arrived right after we left."

Mitchell pointed between Veronica and me. "You two seemed to have everything in hand when we walked into the garage, though," he said.

"We sure did," Veronica said and patted me on the shoulder. "It was all about the teamwork."

"Hey," I said, "has anyone called Pastor Coker?"

"I told them not to bother him," Veronica said. "He needs his rest if he's going to make it through the funeral in the morning."

"If there even is a funeral now," I said. "I'd imagine they'd postpone it."

"We'll worry about that in the morning," Mitchell said. "Now tell us how you knew it was Shane."

I began, "I honestly didn't even suspect him until he was the last person left on my list. Then it made perfect sense."

I explained how he was the one with the information about Suzanne, which meant if she was being framed, he was a prime suspect. He had the opportunity to kill Aidan while the women were taking photos after the wedding, and he was in a perfect position to know when his brother had left the room.

Shane had also confirmed he was the man Aidan had been arguing with in the parking lot after the rehearsal. Darren looked surprised at that revelation, so he must not have even heard about the minor altercation.

Frank popped his head into the room to ask a question about some paperwork. Mitchell stepped out to help him, and Darren offered to bring us some drinks.

The two men soon returned, and I told them the entire baseball bat story, including Shane being in the church building during the time it went missing from the youth room. His trip to "use the restroom" after meeting with Pastor Coker was more likely a foray to retrieve the bat and toss it out the window. Then, when he collected the bat from the outside, he damaged the bush, which Frank had noticed while investigating the car crash.

"Can I stand?" I asked. "This chair is making my hip hurt."

Darren waved his hand in affirmation, so I stood behind the sturdy wooden chair and leaned on its back for support while Veronica filled in some details I had missed. In a few minutes my ankle started to throb from the pressure, so I retook my seat.

The men asked a few questions before I continued with my theories. I explained how Shane could have discovered I was looking into the murder when he talked with Callie in the diner. And I suggested Marty may have called him after finding Aunt Star and me in his shed.

"What about his motive? Did you figure that out?" Mitchell asked.

"I didn't have a clue at the time, but now I do, because he told us."

They didn't let me continue until they sent Veronica out of the room. I figured they wanted to make sure our stories lined up.

Darren said, "Tell us everything that happened tonight. Don't leave anything out."

I detailed everything that had happened since Aunt Star and I left the funeral home. The two men peppered me with questions throughout.

They then sent me out of the room while Veronica recounted her version of events, but they told me not to leave yet.

A paramedic was waiting for me when I left the room. She checked me over, determined I'd just be a little bruised, and headed back out. I sat on a cold metal chair by Frank's desk and sipped my drink while I waited and he filled out paperwork.

I had almost fallen asleep sitting upright when Mitchell called me back in.

When I got settled back into my chair, Darren said, "What you did tonight was very dangerous. I don't understand why you didn't call the police station."

"Would anyone have believed me?" I asked.

He looked down and then said, "I would hope so. Why could it not have waited until morning, at least?"

"I felt compelled to do something as soon as I figured it out. I knew Shane was planning to speak at the funeral, and I couldn't let that happen—for Aidan's sake, but more importantly his parents' sake. Imagine them spending the rest of their lives knowing not only did one of their children murder the other one, but he also made a mockery of it by speaking at the funeral. No. That couldn't happen."

Tears welled up in my eyes, and Veronica patted me on the leg.

Darren said, "That's very kind of you to think of Aidan's parents' feelings, but you still should have called us. I'm certain we would have done something, if you had explained everything like you did just now."

I had my doubts, but I nodded.

"Where was Blair tonight?" I asked. "I would have thought all the commotion would have brought her outside. And where's Aunt Star?"

Mitchell responded, "Mrs. Patrick came out while we were there, but she was in shock. We couldn't get her to say a thing. We called some first responders over to check her out."

"I sent your aunt home when I went to get your drinks," Darren said. "I knew we'd be awhile longer, and I promised we'd get you both back home safe and sound."

"Speaking of which," Mitchell said, "I think it's time to make that happen. Anything else we need from you can wait until tomorrow. You ladies need to get some rest." He scraped his chair back and stood.

We filed out and spent a few moments determining who was taking who home. Frank offered to take Veronica, while Mitchell asked if he could drive me. We agreed to the plan, but as we were crossing the parking lot to the cars, Veronica remembered her car was at my house, so she decided she would ride with us. I offered her the front seat, which left me sitting in the back seat of Mitchell's unmarked police car, with the wire partition dividing me from the two of them.

Mitchell pulled into our driveway and left the motor running. He opened the door for me and then walked Veronica to her car. She declined his offer to follow her home and left the two of us standing together in the drive.

"So," I said, facing him, "will you be going back to Jeff City soon or ..."

"I'll stay overnight a few more nights and then come back for a day here and there as needed to wrap things up, assuming Shane does plead guilty. If he doesn't, I'll be around a lot preparing for the trial." He looked away. "That would also mean ..."

Neither of us could seem to finish a sentence. I finished it for him, "... we can't see each other."

His gaze snapped back to mine. "Exactly."

He stepped toward me, so we stood mere inches apart. My heart thumped, and my hands itched to grasp his waist. I couldn't remember the last time I felt a connection this strong with a man I barely knew.

"We can't do anything that might compromise the investigation," he said in a gravelly voice as his brown eyes searched mine.

Without my permission, one of my hands lifted and pressed against his chest. I could feel his heart rate increase. He moved his jaw from side to side, released a deep breath, and raised his hand to cover mine. I let out a small gasp as our skin touched. I was certain he was about to dip his head toward my own when the yard flooded with light. We both jerked our hands away, he took a step back, and we turned toward the house.

The front door opened to reveal Aunt Star in her soft pink silk robe. She stepped past the storm door onto the porch and shaded her eyes with her hand.

"Sorry!" she said when she recognized the two of us. "I fell asleep on the couch and woke to the sound of car doors slamming. I assumed you were home, but when I didn't hear you come in, I thought I'd see what was going on." She flapped a hand at us and turned to head back inside. "Carry on."

I glanced up at Mitchell and laughed nervously. "While I would love to carry on ..."

"... it wouldn't be a good idea," he finished. He

sighed and leaned back against his car. "You'd better go inside before I change my mind."

I nodded and attempted to put a swing into my step as I walked away from him, but all I succeeded in doing was stumbling on the grass at the edge of the driveway. He caught me by the shoulders before I could fall. I didn't let myself turn to look at him. "Thanks," I mumbled and made my way across the lawn, overly conscious of his gaze following my every step.

Before I opened the door, I turned for one last look at him. He held his hand up, and I gave him a small smile before disappearing into the house.

Aunt Star was waiting on the couch.

"Sorry if I interrupted something out there," she said.

"It's a good thing you did," I replied and plopped down on the love seat. "I'm a witness, you know."

"They'll get the case wrapped up soon," she said. "I heard Shane confess to the murder as he got into the squad car."

"Yes, and then Mitchell will go back to his life in Jeff City."

"Then we can always hope for another murder in Cherry Hill," she joked.

I laughed. "We've only had one murder here in my

lifetime. I don't think there'll be another one anytime soon."

She stood and headed for the stairs. "Maybe a bank robbery then," she said over her shoulder.

"That sounds perfect."

If you enjoyed this book, join author D..A.. Wilkerson's exclusive mailing list!

When you join the list, you don't just receive an email a few times a month. You get book and playlist recommendations, 1980s throwbacks, writing updates, sneak peeks of upcoming books, the potential of joining an upcoming book launch team, and much more. Come join the fun!

To join, go to danawilkerson.com and click "Sign Up."

Find out what Beckett
and her friends are up to
next in Book 2!

Most Likely to Kill

The Class of 1975 is back in Cherry Hill for their ten-year reunion, and they're in for a totally wild surprise. When a classmate is murdered, Beckett is determined to track down the killer, who is almost certainly one of her childhood friends. She knows who was most popular and most likely to succeed, but which of her former classmates is most likely to kill?

Complicating matters, Detective Mitchell Crowe is back on the scene as Beckett's reunion date. However, as he takes the lead in the investigation, their budding relationship is put on hold again. Will this latest roadblock draw the two of them together or push them apart?

Paperbacks available at Amazon.com

eBooks available everywhere

Mystery Journals

Do you want an easy way to keep track of all the suspects or other characters in mysteries? These journals allow mystery readers to record suspects, other characters, motives, means, opportunity, and more!

Available at Amazon.com

About the Author

D.A. (Dana) Wilkerson is the author of the Totally 80s Mysteries cozy mystery series. She has been a professional writer and editor for almost two decades and was the collaborative writer of two non-fiction *New York Times* best sellers: *The Vow: The True Events That Inspired the Movie* (Kim and Krickitt Carpenter) and *Balancing It All* (Candace Cameron Bure).

Dana lives in Oklahoma and enjoys traveling, reading, being an aunt, binge-watching crime shows, and attending Oklahoma City Thunder basketball games.

FIND
D.A. Wilkerson online!

Instagram
@d.a.wilkerson.author

Facebook
@dawilkersonauthor

Tiktok
@dawilkersonauthor

Website
danawilkerson.com

Made in the USA
Monee, IL
10 June 2026

53029988R00156